Grounded

BY THE SAME AUTHOR

Broken In: A Novel in Stories
Tsunami Cowboys

Grounded

A Novel

by

Jadi Campbell

Text Copyright © 2016 Jadi Campbell
Cover Art Copyright © 2016 Walter Share
All rights reserved
ISBN-13: 978-1533343413
First Edition: May 2016
Contact: jadi.campbell@t-online.de
jadicampbell.com

For
Lou

Contents

Monday 11

Tuesday 21

Wednesday 37

Thursday 45

Friday 57

Saturday 105

Sunday 149

Monday 163

Afterword 171

"For what had previously been considered unfortunate necessities, to be played down and apologized for, now became civil and national virtues. As early as the fifties the regimentation of human beings by tapping telephones, opening letters, informal spying of all kinds had been established. ... Also good was the most sinister development of all: the docketing of every kind of information on citizens, not by government and police, but by business firms (on centralised computers), which information was used by police and government. It was a logical development in a society where the needs of industry came before anything else."

— Doris Lessing, *The Four-Gated City*

Love alters not with his brief hours and weeks, but bears it out even to the edge of doom.
— Shakespeare, *Sonnet 116*

Monday

Monday

Vertigo

Tropical fish in the big tank swim away. My image swirls in their wake and I smile. A school of herring in the next tank dart in flashes of silver, and my reflection wavers.

The cell phone in my pocket vibrates, and I walk towards one of the aquarium exits to find a quieter spot.

Rich's voice booms over the line. "Nick! Hey Babe, how you doing?"

"Why aren't you calling at six?"

"We're in Arizona and I couldn't remember which goddamned time zone it belongs to or if this is the state that doesn't do Daylight Saving Time. It turns out *that* depends on whether you're on tribal land. I never did get it straight. Anyway, I called earlier but got your voice mail."

"I was listening to street musicians." I hadn't heard a thing over the noise of metal drums. "You wouldn't believe how colorful San Francisco's streets are. There's a homeless guy down the block from my hotel who writes a new sign every morning. They're pretty funny."

"Nice." My husband wants to tell his own story. "I tell you what – I got vertigo driving us across southern New Mexico. Nothing but low sagebrush as far as the eye can see. I would've given anything for the sight of a tall building! And Arizona, here a forest means saguaro cactus and round barrel cactus with spikes. Christ, even the tree leaves have spikes!"

"Tell Mommy about the rattlesnake!" a boy orders.

"Don't you want to tell her?"

Our son gets on the phone. "Mommy! We went in this cool place called Chir-i-ca-hua." My excited seven-year-old enunciates each syllable. "It has big flat rocks covered in green mossy stuff balanced on top of each other and cactuses – cacti," he corrects himself, "and the sun was hot as heck, and I walked first on the trail up in front and when we went around a big rock I heard a rattlesnake! Their tails *really do* rattle and the ranger in the headquarters told us that snakes are more scared of us than we are of them and that the rattle is a warning to stay away and never ever *ever* touch a snake or pick it up so I ran back and told Daddy and Theresa and Danny about the rattlesnake and we waited on the trail and stood real quiet and watched it for a long time and then it slithered away under a bunch of rocks." The sentence slides out in a stream.

"How exciting, honey! Wow! What did the snake look like?"

"He had stripes and when he slithered he was really long!"

"My turn," Daniella demands. "Hi, Mom! You know how Louie exaggerates a lot but this time it's the truth. The snake was neat." She continues the family report. "We're in Four Corners now. On a reservation," she clarifies. "Navajos and Hopis. Daddy let us stop at a roadside barter post, and Theresa and I got jewelry. Theresa bargained for hers. She got bracelets and I got this ring with a piece of turquoise that has little lines of silver in it. We got a bunch of earrings, too. You can pick out the pair you want."

"Danny! Those were a surprise!" I grin; my oldest daughter is a micro-manager, just like me. Theresa commandeers the phone. "Mom, we're having the greatest time. The trails are pretty easy. Even Dad didn't get blisters. We got a permit for a campfire and this cool ranger sat with us for a while. And, the salsas!" Theresa raves about southwest food.

Rich finally takes the phone again. "So, how's the big city that isn't? How'd the convention go?"

"It was a mix of animal shelter issues and veterinary medicine. I heard a wonderful presentation on reindeer herds. Finnish herders are experimenting with glow in the dark paint on antlers. They think it can cut down on animal deaths and car accidents. They lose four thousand animals every winter in Finland."

"When do you head to Glen Timbrell's? Isn't his son Dylan still there?"

"You ask that every time you call." I stand by a piranha tank, push down my impatience, and try again. "Tomorrow. And yeah, Glen had him all summer. Dylan leaves this afternoon. Turns out I'm taking the same Seattle flight but on a different day."

"Fathers get screwed by divorce, every time." Rich is gruff.

"We don't know the back story." I make myself stop. "Anyway. Timber – I mean, Glen – wants to show me a couple parks. This trip will end before I know it."

"Babe, *forget* California. I've got to bring you to Arizona. Now I know why the guys in the office rave about the golf!"

"Rich, what a surprise…. Well. You have Glen's number and the one for my Seattle hotel, just in case? You didn't use them for tinder to start a campfire? You do still have them, right?"

"In the van where I can't burn them or lose them on a trail." He sounds happy. "Don't even start. If something comes up, I'll call again. When all else fails…."

"We meet at the Space Needle," I finish. "Okay, Ranger Danger. I'm glad you're having a good trip."

"You enjoying being on your own?" Startled, I recognize a combination of tenderness and solicitude. It's the tone he reserves for the kids.

"I can't remember the last time I was somewhere by myself. It's strange to get the chance to think things out."

"I want to hear all about it in Seattle."

"I'm trying," I say. The silence is deafening.

"Well," he finally says. "We miss you and wish you were with us. Kids, say goodbye to Mommy." The rest of the call is taken up in exchanging kisses over the phone line.

My kids aren't tugging on my sleeves stating it's way past time for lunch, or they're thirsty and want sodas, or it's too hot and they need ice cream *now*. I take my time admiring every creature and leave the aquarium pleasantly tired.

Street musicians still play on the corner by the bus stop and I join the listening crowd. Two aging black men play steel drums. Two white twenty-somethings play guitars. A delicate young woman with an Afro and the face of an angel sings, her voice surprisingly deep.

I catch a bus heading downtown. When I reach my hotel, I spot the young man sitting cross-legged by a tuxedo shop two doors down. He wears a red suit coat and dread locks tied up in a man bun. His calm air belies today's cardboard message: *The World is Ending: Two Thousand Years of Predictions Can't All Be Wrong!*

The sleek receptionist spots me crossing the cool marble floors; she hands me my room key. Most of the convention attendees checked out already.

My cell phone vibrates and I read the text message as I wait for the elevator. "Just put Dylan on his plane. Looking forward to Muir Woods and some time with you. Have a good evening," Glen's message wishes.

The elevator emits a subdued ding and the doors slide open. Four businessmen move back to make space. Male eyes look me over.

Once I'm in my room I kick off my shoes and wash my face. I stand at the sink and muse. *Their trip's going really well. In two weeks they only called four times. And just think, wow, Rich is managing a camping trip without me. We won't talk again before Seattle.* As I dry my hands a sensation of lightness fills me. *And my convention is over and I'm by myself, on my own, no obligations to anything or anybody for a few days....*

Monday

Freud's Forest

Hours later I'm still up. The clock on the side of the hotel bed shows 2:27 in red. I'm wide-awake, excited about going to Muir Woods in the morning. When I close my eyes I see trees, tall redwood trees.... How lame can I get? Such obvious phallic symbols.

I run questioning hands over my limbs. I brought unused lingerie to surprise Rich with in Seattle, but until then I'm in a unisexless night shirt. I try imagining George Clooney or Michael Fassbender, but I want a real, accessible body. Actually, I want someone I'm not arguing with.

My hands drop as I relive yet another fight.

"Do you even pretend to talk things over with me first? Now part of your income depends on commissions! In this economy! It's unrealistic."

"The position opened up and I made a decision. Use your imagination, Nick. Think positive." Rich slouched in his chair, his expression stony. "It's a risk we can take, because most people sit on the sidelines. Trust me, out in the field is better than stuck in meetings all day."

I paced the cluttered living room. "Can't you see this puts our family finances at risk? Sales are unstable."

"Why can't you ever relax a little, think outside the box? You don't understand a thing about the business world. You're not in the game." His tone was weary, explaining the rules to an especially dim minor-leaguer.

I threw my hands in the air. "No, of course I'm not in a game." My voice rose. "Rich, for some of us life is serious! I oversee a county-wide animal rescue program."

Rich straightened and waved the inevitable drink at me. "Yeah, right. The resources of abandoned pets and cats in heat. Even better, dogs hit by cars or birds winged by a little twerp with a BB gun. You *oversee* a team of teenagers and otherwise unemployed adults who clean cages. Not the same thing, babe."

"Oh, I get it, I'm dismissed." I looked away. "Just because you think it's a game doesn't give you the right to act like a jerk."

"Get real. Everyone's an asshole sometimes."

I pressed my lips tight not to comment verbally upon my husband's acceptance of the label.

"Especially in business." He pushed it, his anger lit by alcohol. "What, you think Marty Fuller got to be boss by being nice? What sort of dream world do you think I work in? Real life isn't some kind of hamster wheel; it's down and dirty. It's a hands-on proposition."

"Is it?" I banged pots as I pulled one from a cupboard. "How about some hands-on help around the house?" I set the pot on the counter, pushing aside a stack of lunch dishes. The dishwasher was full.

Beyond the kitchen, unfolded laundry waited in a wicker basket on one of the chairs. Our cat Taffy rested on top, her tail hanging over the side of the basket.

Louie had abandoned a puzzle, pieces scattered across the living room rug. The coffee table was covered with soda cans, a jumble of remote control gadgets, the sports section Rich had tossed there, half-eaten sandwiches and crumbs from a bag of chips.

Rich's eyes followed my pointing hand. "You want a cleaner house, clean it! We have kids and pets, and I can live with a little chaos! All of us, and yes I know that includes you, have busy schedules. That's what Saturday morning chores are for. You way over-exaggerate things."

It was back: the sting of familiar guilt. "What's so wrong with wanting a little order? This just isn't what I pictured."

"Nick, the real issue is you're pissed I left Management without talking it over with you first."

"Acts have consequences! Why do I always feel like I'm in

a losing battle?"

"Good question. What do you plan to fight about this time?"

The front door banged open. Louie unleashed Red, who padded over to sniff at Taffy. The cat ignored the dog; not even her tail twitched. Red sniffed again and headed for the coffee table. The dog wolfed down the remains of the sandwiches and licked up potato chips.

"See?" Rich declared. "No need to vacuum."

"When's dinner?" Theresa's question was meant for me, of course.

Danny tugged on her father's arm. "Daddy, help me with my math?"

He leapt up from his chair. "I live to compound your fractions, my child!"

All three kids giggled, and nothing was resolved.

Juggling Acts

I flounder trying to make our impossible schedules work and Rich gets to play the fun parent. This is the deal we made to live in relative harmony. Then, when I registered for my first-ever convention, Rich suggested a camping trip with the kids. I know he did it just to spite me because Rich *hates* the outdoors. But, my objections made me the bad guy.

The noise of a car alarm in the street breaks through my thoughts. I roll to the other side of the bed and turn my mind to Glen Timbrell. He and my brother Randy have been best friends since childhood.

Glen was a skinny boy who continually tripped over his own feet. Randy nicknamed him Timber, a tall figure always about to fall over. The name stuck, and Glen became the jester of our childhoods.

His clumsiness transformed to grace. Timber belly-flopped off diving boards without hurting himself and somersaulted out of trees. He juggled random objects thrown to him without ever dropping one.

He was my favorite out of my brother's friends. Perhaps it was the way he always came over for meals and showed Randy and me how to do flips and hand stands, or the occasional parties we all attended. I sensed that if I needed a brother to protect me and Randy wasn't around, Glen would step in to do the honors.

The last time I saw Glen he brought a bag of DVDs for Randy and regaled everyone with tales from the world of stunt men. Glen trains men and women who are paid to burst into flames, fall from heights, or leap from moving vehicles.

I was pregnant with Louie at the time and Randy and Glen teased me, making me laugh despite the nausea. His wife Janice hadn't said much; their son Dylan played with my two girls.

Janice and Dylan moved to Seattle less than a year later. Randy would only say that divorce was never pretty and it was up to Glen to give the details. Maybe I'll ask him about it when I see him in a few hours.

I picture the acrobatic, funny boy who once lived next door. Smiling, I fall asleep.

TUESDAY

Tuesday

My Alter Egos

The radio clicks on at six. I yawn and stretch. Feeling excited – and enjoying it even as I find myself silly – I shower. I listen to NPR as I dress.

Half an hour later I sit in the hotel café behind the reception area, my suitcase beside me. I savor sour dough French toast with sliced peaches and summer blueberries. San Francisco coffee is blacker and stronger than what we drink at home, and I add more cream.

Around me sit traveling families and couples, a table with professional men and businesswomen in careful suits and skirts, and a group of Japanese tourists armed with superb cameras.

I catch a reflection in the huge mirror behind the buffet table as it reflects back in the windows. My multiple selves raise coffee cups. Nicole Theresa Gleason. Nick to my husband, Mommy to the kids, Nicole to everyone else. Only Glen and my brother call me Nikita. *Nikita: Sister Stupendous of the Church of Chicks. Nikita: Patron Saint of House Pets. Nikita: Mistress of Morning Sickness.* Her title changes, but not the nickname.

My alter egos merge into a forty-two-year old woman of 5'5". She wears a short-sleeved blue shirt over a flowered skirt. Wavy auburn hair reaches below her shoulders. Hers is the direct look of a self-possessed woman, if no longer quite an independent one. She gazes, waiting for me to expand the definition. I shake my head at my reflections. The parameters will suffice. They have to.

I glance out the window to the street. Glen walks down the sidewalk and I recognize him immediately. He wears a green windbreaker and under that a T-shirt with an image of Paul Newman.

He stops before the bum in the doorway to the tuxedo shop. Today's sign reads *The world is ending. Give cash – you can't take it with you!* Glen pulls a candy bar out of the left pocket of his windbreaker. The man reaches up and takes it. They talk, and Glen laughs.

I picture Rich walking down this street. He'd mutter "Get a job". My husband would not shake the hand the homeless person holds out. Glen walks on, not bothering to wipe his hand on his pant leg.

He spots me sitting by the window. "Nikita," he grins as he enters the café.

"Only Randy calls me that anymore!"

The man who hugs me is going gray and his face has weathered lines, but his body is fit.

"Hey, Timber," I can't stop grinning. "Didn't that street guy's mommy warn him not to take candy from strangers?"

"Oh, I'm not a stranger! That's John. He used to hang out in my old neighborhood." Glen pulls out a chair and sits with his long legs tucked under the table alongside mine. "I grabbed some energy bars at the gas station this morning. John needs one more than you will. Or don't you still have enough energy for three women?"

I laugh to cover my astonishment that he knows a homeless person by name. "We'll see how I do today. Do you always give handouts?"

"Never money. Meals, sure. Don't tell me you somehow missed the homeless people living on the streets."

"One for each corner and then some. Where do they come from?"

Glen shrugs. "There's no simple explanation. When Reagan got elected, he closed down public funding for halfway houses and outpatient programs. 'Just get mentally healthy!'" he suggests in a vicious parody. "Anyway, I live in one of the planet's most sophisticated regions – with a Third World overlay. Every place in the US is heading in the same direction."

"Not Grovesville. Small town America is alive and

kicking."

"Amen for that." His face lights up. "Ready for an adventure?" He picks up my suitcase and leads me out the door.

Chaos Lurks

Glen concentrates on morning traffic. We drive through the Marina District and over the Golden Gate Bridge. I twist in the seat, gawking at the view of the bridge and bay receding behind us.

"I never get tired of the views," he answers my unspoken question. He exits into a quiet suburban neighborhood north of Mill Valley. We pull up in front of a green Cape Cod style bungalow. Apart from a plum tree and rhododendron bushes, the yard is grass.

His house has two small bedrooms, a sunny living room and a spotlessly clean, spacious kitchen. The kitchen door has been removed, creating a flow of open space between rooms. A tall mirror in the front hallway reflects light from the glass panes in the front door and a hallway skylight.

"Everything's so tidy!" I exclaim. "Where's the clutter? You don't even want to know what our house is like."

He laughs. "Chaos lurks everywhere… it's tidy because when Janice and I divorced, I noticed stuff stayed where I dropped it. Had to fire the maid. Come on, let me show you where you're sleeping."

I follow him down the hall to where he sets my suitcase in his son's bedroom. It has the unsettled feel of recently vacated space. Careless stacks of comic books and paperbacks fill bookcases. On a corner of the dresser lays a large kite in the form of a cobra, the kite tail coiled on top. Garish posters of contemporary bands cover the walls.

Glen opens drawers, frowning. "I can clean one out if you want to unpack."

I shake my head. "I can live out of my suitcase for a couple days. This'll be like sleeping in a cave anyway. No movie posters for Dylan?"

Glen hangs his head and sighs. "All my good taste and film experience, and he just wants to play air-guitar."

"And it looks like no video games? Louie has stacks."

"Dylan only has one," Glen answers.

We return to the front of the house. The living room contains top end electronics, bookcases, and some pottery. A shelf is covered with pictures. A few show Dylan as a little boy with both parents, but most feature Dylan and Glen. In the oldest photographs Dylan looks a lot like Glen did as a child. In later pictures the boy looks sweet; Glen looks protective. Fatherly, I decide.

In the hallway hang vintage film posters in gold frames and a single oversized photograph. From where I stand it looks like swirls in moving water. Or maybe it's a dark urban skyscraper with wavy glass sides, photographed at a slant angle.

"Ready?" Glen stands by the door.

"I still can't get over how uncluttered your place is."

"Like my life became." He waits for me with a water bottle and wind breakers, and we head out for Muir Woods.

If This Place Could Talk

Sound and light aren't dulled, but relative to the giant trees blocking the sky. Here the world is tans and deep rusty reds. The tree bark is like a hoary pelt or skin. The lowest tree branches begin a story above my head. I crane my neck, unable to see their tops.

I stare with my mouth open.

"Welcome to some of the tallest and oldest life on the planet." Glen sweeps his arms wide open. "Muir Woods is one of my two favorite spots. Tonight I'll take you to the other."

We enter a chapel of trees. Massive trunks surround us, each more than fifteen feet in girth and a hundred feet high. A wooden sign reads *Cathedral Grove*. My eyes travel from the sign up the redwood trunks towards the sky. They're ancient, and I'm a blink in time. I look back at Glen. "Are you feeling what I am?"

"A sense of eternity? God, yes."

The giant trees don't close me in or make me feel small. On the contrary: I feel the freedom from being placed squarely, implacably in perspective. My marital problems and a vision of my inept husband setting fire to the tent by mistake fade. What remains is the peace; the clatter of an unseen squirrel's nails climbing even higher; and Glen's arm as he gives me a companionable hug.

We walk side by side, dwarfed by tree trunks lining either side of the trail. Dust motes hover like wreathes of atoms. They float in shafts of sunlight making their oblique way down to the forest floor.

"I feel as if I listen hard enough, this place could talk."

Glen bursts out laughing. "Don't go cosmic on me. I'm the one who lives in California, remember? But I know what you mean." He halts in front of the stump of a fallen redwood. Red arrows indicate growth rings. "Listen to this. 1929: Wall Street crashed. 999: the first millennia, when the world was supposed to end."

I travel back in time with his words. This tree stood through a thousand years of change. This redwood grove will stand through changes to come. They'll outlast the rise of towers, and their fall.

I trace the rings with my finger. "I'm not a tree hugger, but you know what? For the first time I understand why environmentalists fight for old growth forests. This space belongs to the trees. It's theirs."

"Yeah, we need places like this," he agrees.

"What you said about going cosmic? This place... nothing survives so long without being right for a place and its conditions. What I sense is the rootedness of life that endures longer than an age of man, or a hundred." I'm out of practice with adult conversations that don't morph into arguments and I'm way too earnest, but at least Glen doesn't mock me.

We climb a flight of wooden stairs to the right of the trail. The redwoods keep pace, branches level to our heads. No matter how far we go we'll never climb higher than the crown of the highest tree.

At the top of the stairs I step out on a grassy plain that drops off into the ocean. I'm out of breath, surprised by the shortness of my inspirations. Maybe we climbed the stairs too fast.

Glen breathes normally as he squints, shading his eyes with a hand. There's too much clarity after the woods.

I search, with no idea of what I'm trying to locate. Light glitters on the ocean. Seagulls wheel, too far away to hear or make out clearly. Ditto for the yellow yacht and cargo boats out on the ocean. I experience the brilliance of points of sunlight on the breaking waves; the birds' graceful paths; and the deep color of impossibly old trees.

We share the energy bar and water bottle Glen carried, passing it between us without words.

Mixed Luck

When we get back to Glen's, I shower. I take my time because I can. No kids, no schedule running late yet again, no one knocking on the door needing to use the bathroom as soon as I'm done. After I'm dry and dressed I follow a rich smell down the hall.

He's already set the table when I enter the kitchen. "Hungry?"

"Yes!" Actually, I'm starving.

"Dinner's almost ready." He opens the oven and checks the broiler.

My stomach rumbles. "Do you always think of everything?"

"Hell, yes!" Glen's cheerful. "I'm a control freak. I planned last night with Dylan at the airport. He thought I should take you to dinner, but I figured after a week in the city you've had more good meals out than you can count."

"I resemble that remark," I admit with a smile. Grovesville is no food Mecca. It has other qualities, like being a good place to raise a family. "No thanks. I'm still not much of a drinker," I say when he offers me wine.

He pours himself a beer and I seat myself at the counter as he cooks. I still can't believe how neat his place is. It's not Spartan, it's streamlined male. Sexy somehow. It's attractive. It's… nothing like home. I shift thoughts and make small talk. "Why'd you leave San Francisco?"

Glen hands me a glass of iced tea. "Too expensive. If we wanted to buy that meant a closet in a gentrifying neighborhood. We lucked into bidding on this bungalow. There was a thirty-second foreclosure window of opportunity."

"You made your luck. Luck is never random," I say.

Glen hesitates. "It was mixed luck. I loved the place on sight and Janice hated it in less than a month. Too far from her job. Not enough culture. Pretentious Marin people. Too much traffic on the bridge. The list went on and on. Okay, I either fly to jobs and miss rush hour most of the time anyway; Janice worked downtown. She swore she'd only left Seattle for San Francisco (and me), and didn't leave those cities to sit in traffic jams. Anyway. Maybe it was inevitable she'd want to go back to Seattle."

"What did Dylan say about moving? Our three kids pipe up any chance they get in family decision-making."

"By the time we got around to that discussion, they'd

already left." But he wears a smile when he turns back around. "Dylan spends summers here. I make good bucks as a stunt man."

"What made you go into teaching stunts as well as doing them?"

"An accident that happened because people didn't know better." Glen fills two plates with zucchini and red onions and grilled steaks and jacket potatoes. "Let's eat!"

We sit and eat, and I groan at how good it tastes. "This is great. At our house meals are always last-minute. Rich pitches in with the kids, but he's hopeless in the kitchen. And everyone's fussy!"

"Well, you know what they say: food is love." Glen hastily qualifies, "I mean, cooking's fun."

"Relax guy, I know what you meant. I wish I had time to cook better."

He dishes me up another helping. "When I became single again I discovered if I don't cook, I don't eat. You can get by on take-out food in the Bay Area but it grows old. And when you're dating, being able to cook is a good trump card." He flashes a self-deprecating grin.

My fork hovers at my lips. "Anyone serious?"

He shakes his head. "Not at the moment. I almost moved in with someone about two years ago. Kate wanted babies and I got cold feet. One divorce where I don't get to watch my son grow up is enough."

"I can't imagine what it must feel like not to be there," I blurt out. "Sorry." I make a moue of remorse and drop my gaze. "Divorced dads get the short end of the stick."

"I'm a full-time dad when we're together. We make it work. Some of the dads I know are clueless."

"Not Rich. He's great with the kids and only clueless with me." I clear my throat and it's my turn to flush.

"You sure you don't want wine?" Glen asks.

We can't stop laughing as the topic turns back to our shared childhoods. "Remember those staged fights? You were so funny!" My brother and Glen had choreographed complicated scenarios, trying to recreate film sequences. Randy always got the worst of them.

"God, we practiced moves for hours."

"And you guys and your pot smoking." How often had I caught Glen passing my brother a joint out on the back deck after my parents had gone to bed? On rare occasions I'd joined them. Most of the time I'd snickered and taken a pass.

He shakes his head chuckling and won't let me help clear the table after we finish dinner. "You're on vacation," he says.

I get up from the table feeling like a queen. I go take a closer look at the huge photograph hanging in the hallway. For the first time I recognize the close-up of a falling redwood. The bark ridges and folds resemble ripples in some dark, unknowable body of water or the wavy reflection of a skyscraper. At the bottom is a title in small print: *Timber*. I love it.

Glen joins me in the hallway. "Time for the other place I want to show you."

"Is it far?"

Looking mysterious, he refuses to say more.

Baghdad-by-the-Bay

We drive through empty night streets. The moon is a sliver. Glen parks and we get out, and I follow him around a wooden turnstile. "The park's closed, but they don't need a gate," Glen says. "It's all open spaces."

We trudge up a service road onto a verge of dried grass. The path narrows and I run into something and stumble forward.

Glen puts out a steadying hand. "Sorry – it's tricky in the

dark. Watch your step."

I follow the folds of the hillside and the even pressure of his fingers where they lock on mine. We come over a rise and Glen slows. He leads me to a large boulder and I'm strangely disappointed when he lets go of my hand.

Before us wink the lights of houses, streets, bridges and cars. Tankers with sleeping sailors move across the black ocean. I gaze south where the spans of Golden Gate Bridge rise and beyond them the streets of San Francisco.

"This rock is my spot. I come up here to think things out, or not think at all. This is my favorite place in the world after Muir Woods. It's the reason I left the city."

I sit on the large rock beside Glen as warm evening air wraps around us. He stays silent, content to sit in a favorite place with a friend. I relax into the night, in no hurry. It's so beautiful.

"They call San Francisco 'Baghdad-by-the-Bay'," Glen says after a time. "But it makes me think of Istanbul. In the Turkish night, with lights from Europe to the Middle East, you look across the Bosporus and see literal and metaphoric bridges. Seven thousand years of history, glittering all around you."

I drink in the view from the hilltop and gaze up into the starry heavens. Slow-moving dots of two late-night planes head for their destinies. My breath catches in my throat.

A red pilot light winks in calm pulses from the prow of a heavy ship. It plows the waves in the direction of the Golden Gate. A light from a bridge span winks back, answering the summons of the trawler. My heart thuds as it picks up speed.

Urban scenery lights up and spreads out. The air shimmers. Every atom in my body is in motion. Like damaged nerve cells that had lain dormant as they recovered, it's the reanimation of the part of my innermost being where I identify my self.

All steps have led to this point. I'd searched earlier at the redwood forest for something beyond what I could see. My search ends here. The shadow of a solitary tree on the hillside sways as its leaves flutter and I sway with it. Night insects sing; a slight breeze eddies in this summer night; a tune from a stereo system plays, miles away.

Dizzy, I lean back against granite. The bedrock is still warm from the heat of the day Glen and I shared. I grip the stone. I'm going to crash over the verge down into the waters and drown.

Don't be absurd, I scold myself, *we're miles from the coast, that's a hillside under your feet, that's the locket with tiny photos of your children rubbing against your throat.* I do the only thing I can to stay grounded and not fall off into the vastness of the universe pressing in, urging me out of my skin: I keep one palm on the surface of the boulder so I won't fly away or fall off. With the other hand I take hold of Glen's fingers.

"Nikita," he says quietly.

I rise to my feet.

He pulls me to him and kisses me, and molecules flow between our bodies.

Tomorrow, Maybe Everything

I'm relieved the drive back to his house isn't awkward. We even laugh about the kiss.

"All those years of fantasizing what it would be like. Not *quite* like kissing a sister, but somehow familiar."

"Thanks for understanding," I say. "I mean that. I'd be lying if I said I wasn't a little tempted. And, flattered beyond words. But it wouldn't be a casual affair. I don't do casual, Timber. I don't know how."

He parks in the driveway and grasps my knee. "Nikita, everyone has a corner in their brain where they fantasize about people they're close to, or want to be close to."

"Yes. I keep my corner tightly capped, and I don't intend

to examine it now. It just wouldn't be casual."

He hugs me before we climb out of the car. "Let me know if your situation ever changes."

"You'd be the first to know. Actually, you're the only man I'd even want to tell." The admission surprises me.

Back in his house we move around the kitchen like an old married couple, putting things away. He starts to program the coffee machine for morning.

In the hallway his answering machine flashes. I reach for the coffee pot, upside down to dry by the sink. "You got a phone call."

"Who in the world called so late?" Glen presses the play back button. After a mechanical beep, a man speaks. "Timber? I know it's the middle of the night out in California. But turn on the TV, man. The world's gone to shit."

"That was Randy. What the *hell?*" Glen hits a speed dial number. "Busy." He heads for the living room. "Holy -." That one word contains the horror that just cried from my brother. "Nikita, get over here!"

I join him. The remote control slips from his limp fingers. Glen's staring at the TV and I turn to it with dread. In the corner of the screen a locomotive appears. It travels in a smooth inevitable curve towards a second train. Whistles screaming, they zigzag into heaps.

A bridge leaps up, shaking off cars.

City streets appear. The building signs are written in Chinese but the scene is a déjà vu: a tower's glass windows give back the reflection of wings and body. A plane hovers for a split second like a raptor before it crashes and debris rains down. Chaos; people running. Expanding blankets of oily smoke.

My body goes into spasms as I flinch with each crash. Horror travels down to the tips of my fingers and toes. I smell the stench of scorched metal and liquefying flesh.

Tuesday

Everything fries in the heat released as fuels explode. I hear a bubbling like the pits of Hell.

A shout reaches me. "The coffee maker!" Coffee sputters on the burner coil, streams onto the counter and cascades over the edge. Glen had forgotten to set the timer and the machine had turned on.

I can't tear myself away from the TV. "Computer networks are down. With security compromised, it is unclear whether the train and plane crashes were deliberate or accidental and due to signal failures and loss of steering mechanisms. We don't know if explosions are from bombs or if the explosions are the result of substation meltdowns. No persons or group have claimed responsibility. At present, global authorities suspect a coordinated hacking attack," a commentator says.

My knees are shaking just like his voice. Tonight, maybe the world has ended. Tonight, maybe everything. I reach out blindly, heartsick and seeking safety.

This time, when Glen's mouth and body meet mine, we touch like the last two people alive.

WEDNESDAY

Protection?

I wake deep in the night.

Is my family safe? Where are they? I couldn't reach them last night. *What's happening to the world?* A fourth question follows hot on its heels. *What have I done?*

Facts. *Someone broke her marriage vows.* I force myself to put it in the first person. *I just ended twenty years of fidelity to my husband.* A warm hip rests against mine. *I went to bed with Glen.* My body is warm too, radiant all over.

The act was passion, desperation, denial. The world is ending, and all bets are off. An act with such intimate finality… and I can't take it back.

My brain panics as delayed reactions crowd in. *Protection?* Glen had cupped my cheek gently, saying, "Don't take this the wrong way, but I always use a condom. It's protection for both me and a lover." He has no reason to know I had my tubes tied.

The word *protection* had both comforted and spurred me on.

The questions repeat, faster and faster. *Where's my family? What's happening to the world? What have I done?* I think of Louie, and Danny, and Theresa. I move closer to Glen, holding him in my arms and my children safe in my thoughts.

The Scent of Memories

I wake slowly. *The kids sure are quiet.* I feel a warm male body beside me and for a confused second I believe Rich and I have reunited earlier than planned. I yawn and when an arm goes over the nape of my neck I stretch out towards him before I remember.

Oh my god. This is not my husband.
Glen sleeps.

I stay still not to wake him, but also to recall how I got here.

He feels nothing like Rich. Rich is a bigger man, heartier in voice, affect, flesh. Rich weighs more, but somehow Glen's body is heavier.

Not just his weight on me as he enters and thrusts, although that definitely feels deeper. Needier. Greedier.

Sex with Rich is familiarity. It's affection and two decades as partners and then parents.

In a weird way waking beside Glen feels exactly right. How many mornings as a child did I pad barefoot down to the kitchen and greet Glen and Randy at the breakfast table? How many nights did I pass him on the way to the bathroom to brush my teeth?

Glen is familiar.... I sniff at my fancy. *That's it.* I lean towards him and inhale. Perspiration, semen, dried salt from where our bodies pressed together. Men's shampoo and aftershave with their bracing tonic.

And a whiff of the past. Quietly I turn on my side and breathe him in. It's mixed up, my happy memories of when we were kids, childhood highlighted by all those evenings he lived with us.

Glen letting himself out of the Timbrell's sliding glass door at the back of the house, his face closed against his parents' fights. The arguments drifting over our lawn next door.

A tenderness after his mother left, the careful way he handled his father. A tightness in his mouth and jaw each day after school at the mailbox. He always waited for a letter or post card from her.

Insights tumble out. I can barely acknowledge each before it slips past. I place my hand on Glen under the sheet covering our bodies. I should get out of this bed, right now. I need to engage in damage control. At the very least, I should think about what I'm doing in destroying the basis of trust I founded my marriage on.

But I'm lost in revelations about this old friend, practically my adoptive brother, this man I made love to for hours. We were dying or being reborn in an act to repudiate the terror of a collapsing world. Which fell first, the outside world or the one inside?

Glen stirs and turns, reaches for me. The sheet rises and his particular musk meets me.

I'm dizzy with desire even as reality strikes me like a flare.

Ranger Danger

We rise to a changed world. *Where's my family?* I call Rich's cell phone again.

"Hi, you've reached the Gleason van's glove box!" it laughs.

"Rich, call me, no matter what time it is, no matter where you are," I beg. "I knew it!" I mutter as I relive our next-to-last fight.

"Your plan is, keep the cell phone in the glove box? Seriously?"

Rich made a face at me over the heap of duffel bags. "Nick. The whole point is to separate the kids from their electronic gadgets. It's a wilderness trip. A cell probably won't even work on back trails. Besides." Rich added the final sleeping bag to the stack in the minivan, "We won't need a phone. We'll do fine." He finished and stepped back.

Everything tumbled out onto the driveway.

Rich hunched his shoulders, knowing I was studying him. He swore under his breath as he retrieved the bags.

"Ranger Danger, tell me you're kidding. You never even slept in a tent until you met me." My husband's hapless in what he darkly refers to as the Not-so-great Outdoors. "A camping trip alone with the kids? What were you thinking?"

Rich loaded the Coleman stove into the van. "You spent days organizing park reservations to overlap, just in case. Relax. I hear you, Nick. We'll sign in at every trailhead. We'll survive." His staccato speech and restlessness weren't exactly convincing. My husband is from Brooklyn, and New York City is much more than a state of mind.

"Sunscreen? Snake bite kit? And you swear, no alcohol?"

"Relax!" He kept his flushed face down, busy.

"Hiking in the desert isn't the same thing as sitting on a dock on a lake!"

"I'll call at least once a week, definitely Monday. Six p.m. California time. I have numbers for Glen's place and both hotels in San Francisco and Seattle. You've got numbers for the ranger stations. We'll check park message boards." He ticked off points on his fingers.

"But I won't know what park you're in! You insist on 'seeing how it goes'."

"Like I just told you. That's the point, Nick. Go with the flow, hang loose? And if we love a place we can stay till we're ready to head to the next one."

"What if there's an emergency and I can't track you down?"

His mouth opened, closed. Rich turned his back on me and our tired argument.

"Four, three, two, one," I counted backwards before I followed him into the house.

Rich was in the kitchen opening his first beer. He put out a warning palm. "Nicole, stop. Just stop."

"You could get everyone killed!"

"Stop!" he yelled, and gestured again to Louie and Danny, watching from the doorway.

Why hadn't I insisted harder?

Wednesday

Grounded

All flights are grounded.

I cry out, "What's happening to the world? Where's the president?" Why isn't the leader of the free world speaking, telling us that the heavens aren't going to rain down fire on our heads? I need him. We need to know our leaders are fixing the situation. Is anybody? The unstable air has swallowed the men and women who claimed they safeguard it, and us.

At 4:00 p.m. a rumpled speaker appears before a table bristling with microphones. The press room is packed with officials and reporters. "The president and his cabinet are safe and in a secured area."

"I do not find this calming," I tell the TV.

"We believe this was a single coordinated attack. Terrorists did *not* steer planes and vehicles into targets." The speaker stares into the camera as he emphasizes this point. "This was not the work of religious fanatics. It was a hack on global navigation systems. Experts had considered it possible but not plausible that hackers would grab remote control of cockpits." His tone turns confidential. "We kind of expected a random terrorist was going to crash a plane again. Er…." He stutters, realizing what he's revealed. Eyes down, he reads the piece of paper he placed on the podium. "They took out several air traffic control towers, along with transit stations and transportation hubs."

"Which ones?" a reporter shouts.

The government spokesman's eyes flicker. "Atlanta Airport." He keeps his voice a deliberate monotone. "Bangkok. Amsterdam and Heathrow. Dulles. Frankfurt. The London Underground. Paris Métro. Beijing, where one plane crashed as a result.

"Our top priority is maintaining the rule of law. A curfew is in place. No one on the streets after eight o'clock. Yes, we understand people need to get home from their places of work but if you are on the streets after that time, we will stop you. We urge everyone to remain calm. There haven't been any follow-up attacks. That we know of. We're in contact with our allies and the situation is contained. Everyone can remain calm," he repeats, and ignores the new questions the journalists shout. "There will be another press conference soon. And the Emergency Broadcast System is working. Everyone, stay calm!"

As he turns to leave, the briefing paper slips from his fingers. A camera zooms in for a split second on the list of targets. It's much longer than what he read to us. He scoops the paper back up and hurries from the podium.

In California it's early evening. "How about a walk? We've been staring at the TV nonstop."

Relief shows on Glen's face. As we go out the front door he puts a firm arm around my shoulder, holding me against the side of his body. We walk through a neighborhood of modest bungalows, each probably worth three times what Rich and I paid for our house in Grovesville.

I picture that home. I imagine each family member coming out the front door. I hear the dog bark, the meow of the cat, my husband and children calling my name. My longing for them is so intense I could be hallucinating. I grip Glen's hand, grateful I'm not alone.

We reach the marshes; birds twitter from behind low bushes and reeds lining the sides of the path trodden by walkers before us. I can't see the creatures settling in for the night, but it comforts me to know they're there.

A bridge in the distance crawls with traffic. Are people returning home from offices? Is it the start of a massive headlong flight out of the city?

That night the sex is fierce, a physical release for psychic tensions with no outlet.

THURSDAY

Thursday

Math Problems

Dawn seeps under the window curtains and bleeds from the skylight in the hallway because Glen leaves the bedroom door open. His activities flow from room to room without having to open or close any doors or step over thresholds to reach the different spaces of his life.

How carefully I've shut mine into separate rooms.

The morning report is delivered by a different government liaison. To her left is the American flag; to the right, an oversized world globe. She's the picture of poise in a pearl necklace. "Hackers emptied international corporate bank accounts. No, right now I can't say which ones. Flight manifests around the world were erased. For the time being, the public is advised to remain at home. Or wherever you currently are.... Highways are closing in some places. No, for security reasons I can't identify which ones," she repeats.

All the reporters have the same question. "Has anyone contacted you claiming to be responsible?"

She shakes her head.

"No demands or statements about why the cyberattacks took place?"

She shakes her head.

We go on-line. When I look up my pale face reflects in the computer screen. I've managed to comprehend (in theory only!) why faceless hordes of the impoverished believe radical actions are necessary. I've tried to understand the logic terrorists use to talk followers to their suicides and the murder of innocents. What have believers got to lose? The only bargaining chips they own are their corpses. I can almost understand what drives a human being to strap bombs on his body and blow himself up along with the enemy. Almost.

But these terrorists are the computer-educated elite. They might be the sons and daughters of anyone, from any continent. Two plus two don't add up and my diagram of terrorists falls apart. Within an impossibly short space of time, once again I face the incomprehensible.

Cyber mercenaries are the world's latest terrorists. Cyberterrorists are the world's newest mercenaries. What's happening has nothing to do with religion or political agendas; this is anarchy. We're reaping chaos.

Driven

We go out to find lunch and news. I keep my cell phone on the table, praying Rich will call. The restaurant is abuzz as patrons share information.

"There has to be an emergency clamp down! How else can they get a handle on what's happening?"

"It's martial law in some countries but of course they don't use that term. This is the perfect excuse to implement plans they've had in reserve."

"But who do you target? Nerds in dark rooms, sitting before computer terminals."

When we get back to the house I can't sit still. "This is a nightmare. I have to get to Seattle!"

"I agree, just sitting around is crazy-making. I'll drive you," Glen suddenly suggests. "I need Dylan. I want to be with my son. You don't know it yet, but I'm a control freak."

"You told me that when you made me dinner, when was it? Two nights ago? It feels like a million years."

"It's true," he insists. "Driving up means I control something at least."

I stop pacing. "Timber, do you mean it? I could leave from a nearer airport if airlines start flying again."

"Seattle should be a couple days' drive depending on road blocks. You need to be up there by...."

"Monday afternoon." But he knows this.

"I'm calling Dylan to tell him we're driving up."

I understand his desire to talk to and be with his child. I

wish I could talk to my own kids as I phone my mother-in-law. There's a click as the call connects. "Nina! It's Nick, calling from California. Are you okay?"

"Nicole! I've been sick with worry." Nina talks non-stop for ten minutes. Nervous under the best of circumstances, the tragedy is stretching her capacity to remain calm.

"Nina, your line's been busy every time I've called. Listen, can you go stay with someone?"

"I'm fine. Fine." Brooklyn speaks in each syllable. "The accidents weren't anywhere near here this time."

How like her, to call the terrible events 'accidents'.

"Have you talked with Rich?"

"They're still camping. He might not know yet." I repeat their assumed itinerary, soothing her. "I'm meeting them on Monday."

"Weren't you supposed to go to Seattle *days* ago?"

"Planes aren't flying, Nina. If Rich gets in contact, tell him I'm driving up and I'll meet him as planned. And tell him to call me!"

"Well, Nicole, you're lucky you could get a rental car," she says, and I don't correct her misconception.

Playing by Myself

For the first time in my life I recite a mantra. *Focus on getting to Seattle. Get to my kids.*

Where is my family? To calm myself I picture our last evening together. I'd cooked everyone's favorites. In a household in which pasta is the food of choice, nine times out of ten Louie's dinner vote gets overridden by the rest of us.

"No request turned down," I assured them. "Don't forget, for the next three weeks I get a break from cooking dinner!" I defrosted homemade lasagna for my husband and prepared spaghetti and meatballs for the girls and a breast of chicken with creamed peas on egg noodles for my mini-gourmet. Louie has particular tastes, even at the age of seven.

By unspoken agreement we sat in the kitchen rather than the dining room. The five of us ate at the old wood table as they debated the upcoming camping trip.

Danny wanted to wander the strange shapes of Bryce Canyon and hike in Zion National Park. Louie insisted the trip wouldn't be complete without seeing at least one rattlesnake. Theresa was holding out for the Olympic temperate rainforest.

Rich poured himself another drink rather than say if he had a preference. "I'll let the kids and the weather decide. We've got a lot of parks to choose from. Let's wait and see how we like each place," he suggested again.

Daniella wound strands of pasta and, holding her fork in the air above her face, lowered it to her mouth. The spaghetti reached its target without tomato sauce falling on her white T-shirt. "Mom, can't you change your plane ticket and come with us for the first couple days?"

I smiled as my middle child finished her second helping. "Thanks for the offer, Danny. I wish I could. The conference will start before I'm ready. Remember, I'm on the panel about funding animal shelters. And I only have a few days in Seattle at the end. You can visit the open lands and animals for me." I passed Theresa the bread basket. "I'm jealous you four get to see the Wild, Wild West!"

"We'd visit a ranch if you came."

I shook my head. "Negative. No dude ranches. You guys are going to have *such* a great time!"

Theresa and Daniella made faces at one another. "See, Dad?"

Rich nodded at the girls. "Nick, you've been saying, 'You guys are going to have *such* a great time!' all month. The girls are beginning to wonder if you say it to convince us, or yourself."

"Both," I laughed.

Theresa filled her bowl with spaghetti as Danny grabbed for the serving spoon. "Theresa, you always hog the meatballs!"

"More, honey?" I asked Louie.

He held up his plate with a nod and made an announcement. "I think Mommy wants to play with herself."

My husband cocked a wicked eyebrow in my direction. "Mommy doesn't get the chance to play with, uh, by herself much."

I gave Rich an almost imperceptible shake of my head as I refilled my son's plate.

Louie perched on the seat edge, as usual poised to fly off at the first sign of something new. He'd tucked a leg under his behind.

"Louis, sit in your chair."

He unbent his knee to sit properly and gazed at me.

Kids are smart. Mine always sense when Rich or I – or any other adult, for that matter – gives a phony response. Honesty is the best policy, and my children trust me to tell them the truth.

The whole family waited for my answer.

"Well, Mommy has to do some work, though she does like the idea of playing. But I'll miss you. Hey, who wants chocolate for dessert besides me and Louie?" I asked, and was saved from giving a more honest response.

Eight-Hundred Miles with Road Blocks

I stare unseeing across Glen's kitchen counter. My children will learn about the disaster from someone other than me. At least their father's with them. The girls are old enough to understand a little about what is happening. But, I fret, what about my boy? How will he absorb the news?

Louie vibrates at a higher frequency than most humans.

He has Rich's intensity. Louie throws himself into every game, every temper tantrum. He has no knowledge of boundaries and lives each minute like it's the last.

With a chill a different thought strikes: maybe my son knows something about what's coming in the world that the rest of us don't. I know it's ridiculous, but I can't get rid of the impression. Will he be okay?

It's only when Glen returns to the room that I come back to the present.

We sit and brainstorm. "Okay. It's Thursday afternoon. Looks like planes and trains are grounded for good and that means, road trip. We'll leave at daybreak. I'll check the Web for highway conditions." Glen's computer won't turn on. He frowns and flicks the light switch. "Power's out."

"The second wave?" I hold my trembling hands tight in my lap.

He shakes his head. "The government must have started shutting down grids to pinpoint where the cyberattacks originated." Glen leaves the kitchen and a minute later his car door slams. He comes back with a road map and spreads it out on the counter.

We scrutinize yellow lines.

"1 and 101 up the coast. Eight hundred miles plus from San Francisco." I measure distances out loud. "We'll probably need the secondary roads. Friday, Saturday, by Sunday we'll get to Seattle."

"We'll make it in time to meet Rich at the Space Needle. Let's do it."

"What do we need to take with us?" I reach across Glen for a note pad that reads *Meat. Dairy. Fruits and Vegetables. Sweets.* Quickly I jot. When I finish, on the grocery list are the following: *Batteries. Bottled water. Blankets. Gas can. Flashlight.*

I don't write *A decision has been made for me.* I stare at the list and relief floods me. I can't fly away from Glen and what we've done… and that makes me glad. Unbidden comes this: *the things I never put down in words are emotional.* There wasn't any room for them back when I was sure of myself as a spouse. That surety is gone forever; because of this, I'm ready to feel again.

Glen's shadow blocks my list as he bends over the counter. He kisses me, and the list vanishes. Only feelings remain and I don't consider their shape. I simply exist within them.

Disclaimers

Glen left the television turned on, and it flickers to life as power is restored and the next news briefing begins. The female official informs reporters and the nation that yes, there will be periodic blackouts as they follow the cyberterrorists' trails. "No need for alarm. These won't last longer than three or four hours. We have no way of knowing whether more cyberattacks will follow," she reluctantly admits.

"But unless otherwise noted power outages are now government-mandated," Glen paraphrases.

We pull together a meal from food in the refrigerator, wanting to eat up the perishables. That evening we curl on the couch with our legs entwined.

The cell phone is beside me like a talisman with the ring tone turned up to the loudest possible setting. "My kids," I keep saying. "If I can't reach them that must mean they're okay, right?"

Glen strokes me like a cat, trying to soothe me. "You know," he caresses my ankle, "we should decide what to do about things."

"We did. We leave tomorrow morning." I close my eyes as his fingers move over my calf and up my thigh.

"That's not what I mean, Nikita."

"Let's decide to go to bed," I say, hoping he'll allow me to stall.

The room glows with candles. He leans forward in the chair next to the bed. "I want to see you. Undress for me," Glen repeats in a low voice. "Let's not rush."

The skirt slides to the floor. For a warm moment I can't breathe.

"Nikita." His eyes don't leave my face and body.

I unbutton the shirt and stop, reluctant to remove my bra. I'm a middle-aged mother. My breasts and belly aren't tight, and they sure aren't perky.

At least the underwear I wear is seductive. Rich buys lingerie every year for Christmas and my birthday although I tell him not to. "Try for once to not be so goddamned rational about everything! Be *glad* I still want to see you in something sexy!" he insists.

On my birthday in July, I set down the lavender box and pile of tissue papers. With my fingertips I held up a peek-a-boo nightgown and thong and squinted at Rich through lace cutouts. "It's the same sort of lingerie every year, even if this stuff's pretty. You have no imagination."

My husband got a funny look and turned away.

In the bedroom of a man who isn't my husband, I'm grateful for Rich's lack of imagination. It's my imagination that's been lacking all these years. French cut lingerie was a longing for something else, missing for far too long.

I'd packed the sexy stuff at the last minute, planning to surprise Rich in Seattle. I wear it now, like camouflage, for Glen.

I take off the lacy brassiere; his hands reach for me. His mouth kisses my collarbone and moves lower. "Nikita: Spy in the House of Love. You're beautiful."

It means everything that Glen finds me desirable.

He licks his fingertips before he rubs my nipples. "Marie Antoinette's breasts were so perfect that the first champagne glass is based on their shape."

I break into shaky laughter. "I feel like an extra on a movie set! My name's going to appear in the credits. *Marie Antoinette's breasts: played by Nicole Gleason. No breasts were harmed in the making of this film.*"

He bursts into laughter too and his laugh is a low, deep sound rising from his groin.

"You know she lost her head, right?"

"Now that I get to make love to you I'm losing mine." He strips off his own clothes, impatient.

"What happened to going slow?"

"Later! Later. We don't know how much time we have."

Friday

Friday

What's True?

In an hour Glen and I will be on the road to Seattle. The crook of his elbow rests warm on my hip. The skin between my belly and genitals twinges, sensations his nearness has created ever since we reconnected several days, a thousand years, another life ago. I'm branded by his scent and the imprint of his hands and mouth and body.

What do I know to be true? I can't reach my family in person or on the phone. We're in a crisis of global proportions. I am committing adultery.

These three facts are linked.

I move on to a list of the possible. This might be Armageddon. This could be my last chance for personal happiness before permanent darkness covers the earth.

The list stops while I debate the end of the world. I can't isolate outside events from the damage to my marriage. My life's old patterns have burned away. The fact that I'm even alive overwhelms me.

My body aches, with a literal pain of separation from my children. That feeling is compounded with the piercing joy of Glen's passion. The situation is forcing heightened responses from me to everything,

I'm no longer numb, but I sure am dumb. Should I feel guilty? I know myself, and at some point the old Nicole will. But Nikita's come back.

Nikita: Rebel Housewife. My mid-life crisis arrived right on schedule at age forty-two, but the cyberterrorists.... How can that event arrive right on time? In the end I jumped off an emotional cliff. If I didn't plan it, I sure made a choice.

What's going to rise from the ashes of my identity as a faithful wife? I attempt to look further ahead and my heart thumps wildly. I always keep everything at a nice, analytic distance. *Focus on getting to Seattle. I can think about everything else later.* Glen's hand brushes back and forth across my hip. His fingers curve across the arch of my hip, adding a bit of pressure that makes soft tracks across my skin.

He puts his mouth against my ear. "So you are awake." His erection presses and for a time he blots out the future waiting for us.

Going to Extremes

We're on the road before seven. I stare up the highway, not watching the golden hills roll by. The road is busy but traffic flows without any jams.

No one honks their horns. It's disturbingly quiet, like the silence each morning. It's deafening. *Where are the kids?*

"This is bizarre; I can't believe you're doing this."

"I can," he answers. "Even if it *is* bizarre."

"And extreme," I add.

"How so?"

"You don't think hackers coordinating to shut down the world is extreme?"

"It's tragic and beyond comprehension. But you know what? So is life." A muscle twitches in his cheek and unconsciously he chews on it. "Hey," he suggests, "How about you read? I brought a book. It's in the glove box."

I retrieve a slim hardcover titled *Going to Extremes*. "What's it about?"

"Dealing with extremes. How we survive," he qualifies. A large neon sign warns us that the highway ahead is closed. Glen drops us back in the right lane and signals to exit. He rests a hand on my knee. "Pick the country or place that represents you and your life."

I open the book and scan the table of contents. "The North Pole… yeah that's me, all right."

He startles and gives me a swift look and for a split second I swear I see fear on his face. "The Arctic? You feel like the Arctic?"

"I do. Also, I attended a presentation at my conference on herd medicine. The speaker worked with reindeer. Would you rather I pick somewhere else?"

"No," he says slowly. "Go ahead. We can't get much further from here than the Arctic Circle."

I take a breath and begin to read aloud.

The Arctic Circle

"Snow came down fast and hard. Earlier in the day flakes had swirled in the air. Now it fell from the nighttime skies in an endless thick mantle.

It was beyond cold.

Doug trudged behind Ravna. Sweat pooled inside his layers of long underwear, thick sweater and jeans, snow pants and down jacket. He kept his head down. He was afraid the moisture would freeze, and his face would ice over, and he'd asphyxiate. Doug shivered, tremors running up and down his body.

He needed to halt. Just for a minute or two, long enough to slow his ragged breathing. For a few seconds, no longer. He felt so heavy. Ravna's flash light quivered in the woods ahead of him.

She went on, unaware he no longer followed. "Whatever happens, keep moving," she'd warned.

Doug trembled in the middle of a forest up in Lapland, scared that was the last sentence he'd ever hear.

Blame Putin

The day had begun with his delayed flight to Arvidsjaur. It was a long trip over to northern Sweden where he was scheduled to visit cold weather car test sites. As the plane began the descent Doug saw kilometers of forests covered in snow. They flew over lakes, frozen and glittering. Brilliant daylight reflected on the crystals of fields and fields and fields of snow.

In Arvidsjaur's little airport a dark haired woman held a sign with his name written on it. "Mr. Kendricks!" she greeted him. "I'm Ravna." Ravna wasn't the ravishing tall blond Scandinavian of his hopeful (and male) stereotype. She was ethnic Sami, short with round features. "How was your flight?"

"It took forever! Putin was flying through European airspace back to Russia. We sat on the runway until his plane flew past."

"Your American presidents aren't the only ones who insist on being important."

He placed his suitcase in the back seat and Ravna started the Volvo. Minus six degrees Celsius, the temperature gauge read. "We've got about an hour of driving before we reach Arjeplog. I need to make a few stops. It might be fun for you," she suggested.

Ten minutes later they entered a well-stocked grocery store. Doug wandered down an aisle filled with packages of elk and moose and smoked reindeer meat. The next aisle was stocked with sun dried tomatoes and taco spices.

Ravna explained. "Since Sweden's in the EU, most of the same products are for sale. Plus, local specialties. Reindeer meat doesn't spoil. We can freeze it and thaw it over and over and it never goes bad."

"Mm." Doug picked up a big tub. *Reindeer blood* was written in English along with a number of other languages. "You cook with reindeer blood?"

"Sure! For sausages and puddings. Or dumplings."

"Reindeer blood?" he repeated.

"Up here," she spoke with a mischievous twinkle, "in the Arctic, you eat what's available."

"How interesting." Even to Doug his voice sounded faint. Cautiously he set the vat of blood back down.

He was relieved Ravna only bought bread and cheese and a bag of carrots.

"Okay," she said. "One more stop."

The town was filled with four-wheel drive vehicles and snowmobiles. People skied down the road. Wooden sleds with seated passengers were being pushed by men who stood behind and kicked the sled along in the snow.

"What are those?"

Ravna looked over. "We call them Lappi taxis."

He laughed.

She left town on a straight road and drove through wooded countryside. They passed frozen bodies of water, one after the other. Birches, spruce and pines stretched as far as Doug could see.

A road plow was pushing snow into a bank that was already ten feet high. A black garbage bag hung against the snowbank. Ravna pointed at the bag as she pulled up beside it. "Herders tie these to warn traffic a reindeer herd is grazing nearby."

"Do you know any herders?"

"Want to meet one?" Ravna smiled. She placed the groceries in a pack, and they headed into the woods to find her brother and the other Samis.

Doug Sees Red

When they got back to the road it was already dusk. It began snowing again, flakes that swirled in flurries.

The reindeer and Sami had headed deeper into the forest, Ravna's brother carrying the food she'd bought for him. "They still roam from the mountains and forests to the coast, twice a year," Ravna informed Doug as they trudged towards her car. "Remind me to tell you the history."

Doug was shocked at the cold. *Yes, there was a difference between minus six degrees Celsius and minus thirty!*

It snowed harder.

Ravna drove without talking much, concentrating as the sun went down and the skies darkened with snow and nighttime. She slowed as tall shadows appeared. They came nearer, and in the headlights long poles turned into gangly legs. They passed at a crawl, forced to share the plowed road with four gigantic moose.

Doug let his window down part way and heard soft snorts as the animals kept on going, ignoring them.

"The snow gets so deep that they prefer to travel via the highway too. They can do a lot of damage to a vehicle," Ravna commented.

They passed the animals and the quiet dark took over again. Doug hadn't seen a house or car for miles.

"Wow," he exclaimed. "I've never been somewhere with zero signs of civilization."

Ravna navigated the storm. "Keep a watch out for a light."

Thirty minutes later they hadn't spotted another vehicle or any lights. Outside the car the snow came at a horizontal angle. Beyond the reach of the headlights everything was pitch black as the blizzard sucked all possible illumination from the world. Doug stirred, startled by how sleepy he felt. It was hypnotic.

Somewhere to the left a light winked in the endless trees. Ravna drove slowly for another five minutes, parked, and went around to the trunk. She returned carrying two pairs of snowshoes.

"Have you ever used snowshoes?"

"As a kid. My grandfather had a pair."

She laced them onto his boots. "We don't have too far, I hope. Head for the light."

They left the car and their doors closed with muted thuds. The storm swallowed up sound, too. Ravna pulled her hood tighter around her face and indicated for him to do the same.

Friday

Snow fell in curtains.

"Doug! There's a house up ahead but I can't find the driveway. It's snowed in. We need to cut through the woods, but the trees will give us a little shelter."

She clicked on her flashlight, nodded at him to follow, and clambered up and over the snowbank at the side of the road. Doug scrambled after her, awkward in the snowshoes.

He slid to the bottom of the bank and lumbered behind her. "Use your ankles!" she called. "Whatever happens, keep moving."

The snowshoes prevented him from sinking, but walking was hard work. Inside the woods the unplowed snow lay even deeper. The bare trees offered scant shelter from the storm, their trunks strange ghostly figures as he moved through them.

Doug placed one snowshoe in front of the other, trying not to stumble or lose sight of Ravna. She moved on ahead, encased in white. The light source seemed nearer. As he tried to keep up his thoughts wandered. *In film scenes, people are warned to avoid the light. In all of them Death waits in a tunnel, calling from the other end.*

Snow kept falling as time collapsed. Doug looked down and saw, stupid, that he'd vanished. He'd transformed into a staggering humanoid smothering in thick snow.

The light was brighter. He wondered, *does no sensation in my fingers and toes mean my organs are safe, or will they go numb next?* His lashes stuck together and he could barely make out Ravna's shape. He trudged in her wake.

They left the shelter of the trees and Doug stumbled atop a high expanse of white, following the path she carved on the sea of snow. Something solid rose; a Fata Morgana? In the part of his brain that wasn't exhausted and frozen, Doug recalled that Arctic explorers had imagined walls of ice rising before them.

But this apparition wasn't white. He saw red, a wall of

red, and then he ran into the side of the red house.

Follow the Borealis

She poured him a cup from the thermos on the counter. "Sugar and milk?" She spoke calmly, as if entering the house of a complete stranger and making themselves at home in the kitchen were the most natural things in the world.

Doug sipped at the coffee; his skull hurt where he'd smashed into the house wall. He suspected his left shoulder would join his head soon.

Ravna poured a second coffee for herself and sat in one of the light beech wood chairs with an enigmatic smile. Maybe it was encouraging. "I promised earlier," she began, "to tell you about reindeer herding in the Arctic Circle. I'll tell it now.

"Finns thought Northern Lights were the lanterns Sami carry as we follow our herds. People in parts of Sweden and Norway said the aurora borealis is the reflection of millions of silleblixt, what you call herrings, swimming in the sea.

"Scotsmen call Northern Lights 'Merry Dancers'. In the Middle Ages, when people saw a red borealis, a war had started. Red lights meant death and blood spilled in battle.

"My people believe everything in Nature, from animals to minerals, possess souls. The Eskimos say, the aurora lights up the trail of the afterlife. It's a dangerous narrow path souls have to take to leave dead bodies and head to Heaven. We believe the aurora is a place where the dead stay. Above all, it's for people who die violent or premature deaths. The aurora is a place for mothers who die in child birth and their unborn children, or suicides, or people killed in war or murdered."

I stop reading, envisioning the trip being taken by the souls caught in cyberterrorism. I hope their path is a clear one. Maybe life consists of moving between extremes, whether of birth, or death, or the task of surviving the trip from one to the other. I need to clear my throat a few times before I can continue.

"But I was going to tell you about reindeer," Ravna went on. "Sami use over four hundred different words for reindeer. According to legend, we made a pact with them. Symbiotic survival. We feed and protect them from predators, and they help us survive. It's winter five or six months a year. With so few resources, well, we're resourceful. We use reindeer pelts for clothes and tents and blankets. Their hairs are hollow: perfect heat insulators. Did you notice the pelt strips on the bottom of your snowshoes? Traction."

Doug looked over at the front door where she'd set the snowshoes before they entered the house.

Like magic, the door swung open. A tall Swede lowered his fur lined hood and stamped to remove as much snow as possible before he took his boots off.

"Är din bil på väg?"

Ravna and the man with light blue eyes talked for a few minutes.

"Jan Gundrinsson," the man added.

"Ravna Engström." She shook the hand he offered. The two turned to Doug. "He says, 'Is that our car out on the road?' We stopped short about a hundred meters from his driveway. But we wouldn't have seen it anyway; the drifts are too high.

"This is Doug Kendricks," she introduced him.

Doug got to his feet. "We got caught in the storm and your house was the first shelter we came to. We didn't mean to trespass."

Jan was already waving a dismissal. "More coffee?"

Baffled, Doug began to stammer.

Jan and Ravna broke into laughter. "We don't get many

break-ins here," the big man assured him in perfect English. "Too inbred. Everyone knows everyone else. But we look out for one another. No one turns off their lamps. When you get caught in a storm the only thing to do is head for the light. We don't lock doors for the same reason. You never know when you might need to get out of the cold and snow."

With pleasure the two Swedes took turns reciting.

Ravna: "It'll melt in May."

Jan: "In the spring we truck snow out of town, or basements flood."

Ravna: "Once the ground thaws, Sweden breeds the world's worst mosquitoes."

Jan: "Fall lasts about two days and then they start getting short again."

Ravna: "Further north, it gets dark even earlier."

Jan: "We own more snowmobiles than cars. It takes forever to airlift you out if you have an accident."

Glen makes a strangling noise. He's gone as white as the snowbanks in the story.

"Are you okay?"

He nods and moves his right hand from his throat, waving for me to continue.

I look at him uncertainly and finish the chapter.

"'I bet you're wondering why we stay. Why? Because it's beautiful and peaceful. No stress, no crime, the wilderness as your back yard, and skies that bring the Northern Lights. The Arctic Circle is a place completely ruled by the environment. You adapt or move; there's no other choice. Mother Nature has the last word.'"

Get Back in the Truck

Glen is silent when I close the book. "Well," he finally says. He sounds reluctant. "That's certainly a break from

Friday

reality."

"It is reality, just not the one we're stuck in. What I wouldn't give to escape to a world like that for a little while."

He closes his eyes tight for a second.

"Timber? Are you *sure* you're okay?"

He pats my knee with his free hand but his thoughts are elsewhere. "Just thinking about Dylan.... So. How is your life like the North Pole?"

I stare out the window. I'd missed the scenery, too caught up in the wintry depiction. *Seriously? It matches the way my life felt. Nikita the Ice Queen, Nikita the Frigid.* "You can't choose," I say. "There's no room for mistakes." *The worlds of mom and lover are poles apart. When you choose one over the other, what's at risk? How do you claim your own life back? Can you?* "You can't assume you'll survive. Imagine a place at minus thirty degrees and dark, and people survive by looking out for one another. Symbiotic relationships. Wow, what a concept. Why can't the rest of us do that, instead of what we *are* doing?"

Hurriedly I change my train of thought. "Louie still believes in Santa Claus. He thinks Santa and his elves live up at the North Pole in igloos. For me, it's the idea of herds roaming without borders, national or otherwise." I add a last, slow remark. "I like thinking that even if you're forced to live as an Ice Queen, life can carry on with dignity."

Glen's expression is gentle. "We should find a place to stay before the curfew. And we need food for the road tomorrow."

We enter a little community. He drives while I keep an eye out for a store. At last I spot a large white building with a sign out in front that simply reads, *Market*. It's the first grocery opportunity we've seen and the narrow lot is full. We pull in and park.

The market bustles with stockers refilling shelves. Everyone's buying bottled water and canned goods, but a lot of carts contain expensive cuts of meat. *A condemned world's last meal*, I shiver.

Voices float disembodied from the aisles on either side of us.

"...so they can enforce the curfew...."

"Some prisons had their electrical doors pop open. It's chaos. Who knows how many prisoners managed to slip out?"

"It was an inside job."

"More like an international one. Countries are internetted. I mean, look at Europe. Security systems fell like dominos."

"...hospitals went to backup generators. Now they have to recheck patients and administer drugs individually. Dosage information, scrambled."

"What if sperm banks got ruined? Crap! There go my three billion donations," a male voice complains.

We laugh aloud, grateful for a little levity.

I wrinkle my nose when Glen places a plastic container of marinated tofu salad in the shopping cart.

"It's good!" Glen squeezes my fingers.

"*So* Californian," I smile. Glen's hand in mine relaxes me.

"They don't sell tofu in Grovesville?"

"They do. I'd buy it, but Rich and Louie won't eat it." I stop with the mention of my husband's name. I still don't feel guilty. Instead, I keep imagining my family camped in a desert. I hope they're blissful and unaware of unfolding events.

We pick out crackers, bread and sliced meats and cheeses, nectarines and bananas, bottled water, chocolates. It's a relief to occupy myself in the mundane task of planning a picnic. Grocery shopping appeals to smell and taste instead of my overstimulated powers of imagination.

After we pay Glen and I stroll out to his BMW, each of us toting a grocery bag. We put them in the back seat. I get in front, buckle my seat belt – and can't recall a single purchase.

"Did we get chocolates?"

Glen runs his hand up and down my leg. "Who cares? I know what I want for dessert!" He has a wicked grin on his face as he starts the car.

A Ford pickup and a sedan approach from opposite sides of the lot. Both speed up. The sedan refuses to pull over and give the wider vehicle room. The drivers screech to a halt at hard angles.

Glen pulls up to within a few yards. "Now what?"

A short blond guy climbs out of the pickup. He's about thirty years old and wears a hunter's vest.

The older man behind the wheel of the sedan lowers the window, his face red. "Got a problem?"

The pickup driver gives him the finger.

The sedan door barely misses the truck owner's knee as it bangs open. "Let's talk," the older man suggests.

"Move!" the first man demands.

"Don't tell me what to do. Move the truck." The older man's tone is level; his voice is cold. He steps closer.

A line of cars grows and horns honk.

The truck driver slowly tugs the edges of his vest down, places both palms on the chest of the sedan owner, and pushes.

The older man stumbles back. "You want to get into this with me?" He bangs an open palm down on the hood of the pickup.

"Don't touch the truck, dick weed."

All around us trapped shoppers lay on their horns. "Take it somewhere else," drivers shout.

People climb out of their vehicles, doors slamming. A man by a blue SUV keeps yelling as he reaches for his shoulder holster.

"Oh my god, Timber, he's got a gun!"

Before I realize what's happening Glen is out of the car. He lopes over to two men screaming with their faces inches apart. He shoves forward and wedges himself in the middle of the fight.

"Get back in your cars and drive away. Peacefully! You need to get back in your cars and chill the hell out! I'm serious!"

The pair stop exchanging insults and stare bewildered, and then both attack Glen. They throw punches that Glen nimbly dodges. The bigger guy swings again and Glen ducks. His partner's balled fists whirl through the air and land – nowhere.

This is the sort of ballet Glen performs at work where it's make-believe. Here, it's surreal. The scene freezes with a pair of strangers facing Glen like they've become a team; a nameless grocery store; vehicles at odd angles blocking the exit of a parking lot.

"Do like the man says! Get a grip! Get back in your cars!" Voices are louder as people add comments in the hope this nightmare can end, unlike the larger one we share. The SUV driver has his gun out. Everyone watches Glen intently.

Glen is motionless, body poised for whatever might come next.

Motors idle, angry. People wait, some of them on their anxious way home to eat dinner with their families. Others will turn on televisions in the hopes of a more informative briefing. And the rest will draw blinds to shut out the dangerous world and sit in the dark.

The sedan owner mutters something at his feet and everyone climbs back in their vehicles.

PTSD

Glen's door thuds shut.

"Timber." I put a hand on his arm.

He won't respond to my touch, but doesn't move away from my hand. "I need a minute here," he rasps, twitchy. He stares unseeing past the book on the dashboard.

I stroke his arm. The diamond in the band on my ring finger glints as a streetlight flickers on.

Is he crying?

Glen encloses my wrist with his hand, both to stop my stroking and acknowledge it. An eerie mind-reading is at work. "The last time I cried was years ago. This is road rage."

"You haven't cried since?"

The entire street lights up.

"I haven't been this upset since. It seems like we're having a collective nervous breakdown."

The last cars pull out of the parking lot, people's faces illuminated. Everyone looks grim. They have every reason to.

Where were You

We check into a roadside motel a few miles down the road and order dinner in the attached diner.

"Is there any new information?" People look up from their meals at our question and pass along the latest facts, or rumors.

"The last briefing, the speaker said, the government's got fuel supplies under control. No worries about lines at gas stations."

"I don't care what the government's claiming. I told my husband, go fill every canister we've got while the getting's good."

"The attack came from embedded commands, the single most destructive virus ever written. Hackers used the NSA's own schemes against them. Everyone's paralyzed. You can't make decisions or adjustments if there's no data coming in."

"They hacked into data bases just long enough to push the right buttons. I won't get home anytime soon, will I?" The speaker sounds British and his comments aren't questions. "Bloody NSA keeps pretending their plans couldn't get highjacked. Same for our British GCHQ. Bloody…. Sorry, no offense. Nothing against Americans." He stares into his beer.

"None taken," the others assure him. "It must suck to be so far from home during this."

"At some point they'll get it sorted out and the planes and trains will start running again. You'll get back."

"I suppose." He agrees without enthusiasm. "In the meantime, just like here the authorities are making people stay off the main arteries in case they have to move troops."

"And respond to home-grown terrorist groups. Christ, they're jumpy. So far no one's taken credit for the attacks."

"Can we change our order to take-out?" Glen mutters.

I don't want to remain in the brightly lit, red and white checked café either. "Have you noticed that as much as we always ask for news, we never join any of these conversations? I feel like until we're with our kids again, it's just you and me."

"Just you and me, Nikita, traveling through a world that doesn't make sense anymore. That's it in a nutshell," he agrees.

We eat fish and chips back in the motel room, surprised that a meal can taste good. But it's hard to enjoy when you've traveled too far.

Where's my family? Where were you and what were you doing when you found out President Kennedy was assassinated? That's the defining question of my parents' generation and their world changed forever. In 2001 the defining question changed, different before and after markers. Where were you and what were you doing on Nine-Eleven? All you have to mention is the date.

For my three kids the question will be, where were you and what were you doing when you found out cyberterrorists had shut down the world?

Where was I, and what was I doing? I was going to bed

with a man who isn't my husband.

Leaping into the Void

I turn on the television and objects in the news footage drop.

"What are those?" asks Timber.

A news ticker starts to flow at the bottom of the screen as a reporter speaks. "This afternoon, a new incident in Malaysia. People jumped off the Petronas Twin Towers in Kuala Lumpur. Tragically, when an elevator jammed and the fire alarms went off, they assumed a new attack was under way...."

I want to throw up. "Can we turn that off?" I croak.

Glen moves swiftly towards the television.

"I can't take it. I mean it. Oh my God. They thought they were going to burn up. What goes through your mind if you'd rather jump out a window? Can you imagine death by burning?" I turn away to stop myself from crying. "I'm really sorry," I say, but I can't read his expression.

Glen turns off the TV and all at once the hairs on my arms rise. The air is fraught with words about to be spoken.

"Nikita: Witness to my Extreme World." He hesitates, but his face clears. "I want to tell you why Janice and I got divorced. It was a Saturday morning, and it was windy."

Stunted

Glen stepped back from the photo.

Janice scowled at him or the oversized photograph, or both.

He tried anyway. "What's for breakfast, gorgeous?"

"See for yourself." She fiddled with the buttons to her bathrobe, avoiding his outstretched arm. "So much for family night." His wife slipped past him in the hallway. "One time,

Glen. Just once, can't you get home when you say you will?"

"I'm a stunt man. That's what I get hired for: to do movie stunts. And some shoots take place at night."

"When you promised to spend the evening with us *watching* a film."

"We're lucky the shoot's even in the Bay Area."

She tightened the terrycloth belt and glared at the falling redwood and its title. "Can you stop being Timber for a while?" With the question she headed to the bathroom.

"So what's for breakfast?" he asked again, his voice raised.

The bathroom door slammed behind her.

Glen checked, but Janice had cooked pancakes and bacon for only herself and Dylan. Glen made toast.

He drank coffee and lifted his shirt. His side was a blooming bruise. He'd spent the evening performing falls in clouds of smoke. The crew had used every last squib.

He stood, not too stiff, and got another cup of coffee.

Winds battered the house. At least he and Dylan could fly that kite they got in China Town.

His reveries were interrupted by loud bangs. *Exactly what he needed more of.* He turned to the window just as trails of smoke spiraled out of sight. Bang. Bang! Screeching whistles came next, followed by what sounded like ten lit strings of firecrackers. Bang! Bang! Bang! Bang! Bang! Bang! Bang! Bang! Bang! Bang!

Glen groaned and went outside to look.

Snap, Crackle and Pop

Dylan crouched with a group out in the street.

A smoke bomb went off as Glen asked, "What's going on out here?"

"Fourth of July." The kids gave the obvious response and

Friday

turned back to a box.

"Isn't it a little early for fireworks?"

"My dad says it's okay as long as we keep them away from houses or cars," a brown skinned boy explained.

Davy, Glen recalled.

"We've got bottle rockets!" an excited girl bragged. *Michelle*.

Fire crackers popped, each bursting in Glen's brain. *Cripes. Whatever happened to sparklers?* "Which one of you kids is responsible for safety?"

Davy raised his arm.

"Don't set those off in the road. Bring the box up on the lawn."

Davy and a friend grasped the cardboard box. Once they set it on the grass, Glen supervised as they lit more crackers.

A little boy with dirty blond hair tugged on his shirt. "Hey, Mr. Timbrell, walk on your hands for us?"

"It's cool how you walk upside down!" someone cajoled.

Children surrounded Glen, who removed the loose change from his pockets. "Give me room."

"Do some flips?"

Glen obliged with a series of forward flips and reversed to come down on his hands. From upside down he smiled at five boys and three girls.

"Yay!"

"Yay!"

"Way cool!"

They cheered and clapped as behind them Dylan reached into the box. Only Glen, blood rushing to his head, saw the lit match a bigger boy held to a bottle rocket. At the last minute he threw it and the rocket arced wildly through the windy morning before it fell and landed in the pile of fireworks.

Dylan was turning, a Roman candle clutched in his hand.

Glen flipped upright and sprinted across the lawn as he

yelled his son's name.

What's Your Emergency?

Dylan wouldn't stop shrieking. Flowers in the yard withered, writhing away like a spool of film played backwards. The lawn smoked in places.

"Dylan, it's okay, I'm here. It's okay." Glen brushed a trembling hand over his son's forehead. "I'm here. It's okay, I'm here."

Dylan gripped him and moaned.

Janice came down the steps with blankets in her arms and wet hair down her shoulders. Her robe flapped open without her noticing. "How bad?"

Glen swallowed hard and went cold despite his own pain. Tears coursed down his face. "It looks like his shoulder blade and back. Bad."

"I called 9-1-1. We'll have to keep him still till they get here." She spread two blankets on the lawn. Gently she lowered Dylan down on one of them. "Dylan, listen to Mommy. Be very, very brave and stay quiet until the ambulance comes. I know you can do it, we're right here with you. Glen, you need to lie down, too."

He looked confused at her hands tugging on his right elbow.

"Sit," she ordered. "You're in shock. Glen, you burned your hands. You're in shock," she repeated. "I want you to lie down on the other blanket." Her crisp words willed him to comprehend.

Glen's vision telescoped and the lawn expanded. The world moved away from where he stood swaying. He turned, and the hard ground rushed up to meet him.

Friday

When the Smoke Cleared

He woke in a hospital bed. After a few disoriented minutes he made out a doctor, waiting for him to swim up to consciousness. Glen didn't remember the trip to the hospital. "My son?" His throat hurt and his head was too heavy to raise. Glen dropped back on the pillow.

The doctor pushed glasses up his narrow nose and ran a hand over salt-and-pepper hair. "I'm Dr. Carter, and you are a *lucky man*, Mr. Timbrell. Under different circumstances I'd shake your hand."

Liquid flowed down into a catheter taped to Glen's wrist.

"You burned both hands. You have partial thickness blisters that are going to break. But most are superficial heat burns: those should start to heal in about a week. The real depth isn't easy to judge or even obvious, so we'll watch them."

Glen shifted his right arm and grunted. His bandaged hands hurt like hell.

"I wrote you a prescription for pain killers and Silvadene salve. The pain will ease up in a couple days. You'll need spoon-feeding for a while." Dr. Carter's slight smile vanished. "Do you remember being brought in?"

Glen tried to shake his head but movement made him dizzy. "No." He closed his eyes. "What about Dylan?"

Dr. Carter moved the white bucket chair away from the catheter tube snaking down and seated himself. He read from one of the charts he held. "Dylan has superficial and partial-thickness burns across the top of his shoulders. No injury to the spine or head. One full-thickness, third-degree burn over his left scapula. That one is by far the biggest. The team will debride the burns and monitor the situation to determine if he'll need a skin graft."

The world swam in a fog of painkillers. Glen nodded cautiously and swallowed hard, his skull pounding with the mother of all headaches. "Is he in pain? Will the scars be bad?"

"This is hard for a parent to hear, but your son's greatest advantage is his youth. Young tissues heal the fastest. As awful as it sounds, in this country alone 250,000 children get treated for burn injuries each year, most of them caused in household accidents. Dylan's burns affect ten percent of his TBSA. Total body surface area. No laryngeal edema. Throat area swelling. He's going to need continued supervision. Your wife will take over the home care duties."

"Wait. Janice is going to quit her job? But I'm here."

"Exactly."

"Exactly?" With difficulty Glen turned his head towards the new voice. Janice sat on the other side of the bed, arms crossed tightly over her chest. In the effort to focus on the doctor's words Glen hadn't noticed her sitting there.

She wouldn't meet his eyes. "Exactly. You know what? I watched the whole thing from the window. Those fireworks exploded because you had to show off. It's a good thing all the kids except Dylan were standing by you, watching you walk on your hands. While our son was reaching into an exploding box." Her next words rushed out. "I want him treated in Seattle."

"The Bay Area has some of the best medical facilities in the world!" Glen's head throbbed.

"I can stay with my parents and my family will help me out."

"You don't think I'm here for you and Dylan?"

"You're always off on movie sets."

Dr. Carter held up a hand and Glen noticed black hairs on the back of it. "The most advanced Burn Unit is in Harborview Hospital in Seattle."

"Give him the form." Janice struggled to keep her voice steady. "Sign the papers, Glen. Make an X."

The doctor sifted through medical reports. "This is the

release form. We'll airlift your son to Harborview. Mr. Timbrell, you should remain here. You have a concussion; you hit your head pretty hard when you passed out. Dylan will be all right. If you consent, he'll receive care at one of the finest Burn Units on the West Coast."

Keeping Secrets

I go to Glen and he pulls me onto his lap. We hold one another. "Does Randy know?"

Glen nods *yes* into my shoulder. "Randy's good at keeping secrets. I don't think I would have minded if he'd told you."

"He flew out to see you." My brother had made a sudden trip to the Bay Area, saying he needed a break and work could wait. "Randy boarded his dog and cats at our kennel and I drove out to his house to bring in his mail. He never did explain why he took a vacation so spur-of-the-moment. Now I know: it wasn't a vacation at all."

Glen nods another yes and resumes his story.

The Line Starts Here

Glen dictated the number and Randy held the cell phone to his ear.

"Janice, stop being defensive. What's done is done. You did what you thought best. Harborview is the right place as long as Dylan needs intensive care. We can talk about what to do later once I'm there. No, I'm not going to wait until I can use my hands again. No. I'm flying up, now." Glen listened for the next few minutes. "He's my son too!" He listened further. "Get serious. San Francisco has decent therapy centers." The strain of the past days scratched out. "It's not like this is the middle of nowhere!"

A dull dial tone buzzed and Randy turned off the cell with his eyes averted.

"Fuck!" Glen banged his bandaged hands against his thighs.

"Not good?"

"Janice is convinced Dylan needs quote 'stability of medical care', unquote. It's an excuse to move back to Seattle. What I need is incidental."

Randy cancelled his flight home. "Save your breath, Timber. I'm going with you," he said, and wouldn't listen to any objections. They flew to Seattle and drove to Harborview Medical Center in a rental car after three attempts to reach Janice.

Together they walked through hospital corridors to a long waiting room. Injured people and family members filled most of the room's chairs. Tired security staff eyed them. *Why are they all wearing gloves?* Glen wondered.

Two security officers set a homeless man down in a wheelchair. He slumped forward as clotting blood dripped from his beard. Glen realized the officers wore the gloves to protect themselves from contact with body fluids.

Policemen entered, escorting an unconscious young man on a gurney. His sweatshirt was soaked red.

Randy spotted an arrow pointing to a sign. *Trauma Unit. Line to talk with the nurse starts here.* He ignored it and collared the next staff person to walk by. "Can you direct us to the Burn Unit, Dr. Sullivan?"

The woman with russet hair and a nametag stopped short. She ignored the rugged, handsome Randy and assessed Glen's bandages. "Are you expected in the Burn Unit?"

"My son's there."

"That way." Dr. Sullivan pointed and walked off. "Hey, Murad! Wait up."

A dark-haired man with a dangling earring and a lab coat halted. His right hand rested on a pneumatically propelled x-ray machine. He turned, and his saturnine expression transformed with a brilliant smile. "Shannan! Just the sight to brighten the end of my shift. I've got slips for three more chest x-rays. When those are done I'm gonna go home and sleep till Friday."

"Oh, no you aren't. Not before I see your new slide show of that month you spent on Bali."

"Promise you'll buy me a beer."

"Done! You're on!"

"Only for you, sweet Shannan."

The two laughed and vanished from sight when they turned a corner.

Glen and Randy continued silent down the corridor. They were oddly calmed that the hospital personnel might flirt with one another, take trips to exotic locales and joke about sleep deprivation.

Glen thought, "I sure hope Dylan's medical team is made of people like them." He held the hope for himself, bracing instead for what waited on an upper floor with a sign reading *Burn Unit*.

His Second Home

Randy drove Glen over each morning and picked him up in the afternoon. He didn't leave Seattle until Glen's hands healed.

Watching the hospital staff remove bandages and clean the burns became the defining elements organizing the life of Dylan and the lives of his parents. Even when he returned home to California and came up on weekends, Glen only existed inside those sterile hallways.

The ward became his second home. He no longer blanched walking by the Burn Unit's Pediatric Intensive Care Unit. But imprinted forever was the first time he saw a crib in a wheeled cage. The rational part of his brain understood this allowed the medical personnel to move a critically injured infant without having to touch the baby.

The parent in him screamed at the sight.

He learned to endure sessions in the burn patient bathing room. He stood by as Dylan lay beneath the two water hoses hanging from the ceiling. When had he first arrived at Harborview? Glen tried to gauge how much time had passed since Dylan's accident and gave up. His powers to calculate had collapsed along with his son's burned tissues.

Dylan's doctors approached them. "Mr. and Mrs. Timbrell, we'd like to suggest a special form of therapy for Dylan. This is cutting edge, and best of all, it doesn't involve drugs."

The computers in every room reassured him. Machines supported Glen's deep need to believe that enough technology can atone for things like a box of fireworks and human error. "What are you proposing?" Glen asked.

One of the doctors held up a helmet.

Blah Blah Blah

The plane to Seattle left late and then sat on the runway for three hours. When Glen finally reached Harborview and stepped off the elevator into the Burn Unit, he was exhausted.

Today no family members were sleeping in the waiting area. Only one person stood at a window. She stared out in the direction of Smith Tower, once the tallest building west of the Mississippi. Beyond it, a ferry sailed away in the waters of Puget Sound.

The woman had pulled her dark hair back into a sloppy, careless ponytail. She reached up an absentminded hand to tuck wayward strands behind her ears. Hair fell back down over her eyes as soon as the hand was gone.

Brown slacks hung in creases around the backs of her knees. She'd probably pulled on the pair of pants from where she'd dropped them on her bedroom floor. Even her simple beige T-shirt looked tired.

It was the outfit of someone who'd begun the slip into despondency. Perhaps she toyed with the idea of moving over into the more dangerous territory of despair. She looked like nobody Glen would want to be caught with in a crisis situation.

She turned, and it was Janice. *My wife,* Glen amended. *That other person, the one you're supposed to build a mutually supportive life with if you're married.* He had no desire to go to her. "Janice."

She looked at him and her face was blank.

Both stood, unwilling to breach the cold four feet of space between them.

"You're not in with Dylan and Doctor Erdogan? How's Dylan's appointment going?"

"They're checking the scars. I hate it. He goes into another world and turns into a zombie."

Glen dropped into the nearest chair. "They warned us. Sometimes wounds need to be reopened in order to heal. That's not how Dr. Erdogan put it, but it's what he meant. You can't know if they need to do that today. Bodies don't always heal the way we expect they should, not if it's a difficult injury, especially burns. Dr. Erdogan told us this, months ago," he said, trying to console himself as well as his wife.

"I can't watch. It's horrible."

"Yes. It is." Glen stood back up. He stared at this woman who slouched before a panoramic view. "But it's Dylan who needs a way to bear it. Not us."

"What's *that* mean?" She spoke eagerly, grateful for the gift of an open fight and not one with herself and her thoughts. "I'm the one who stays with him round the clock."

"And why is that, Janice, just why might that be true? Maybe because you brought Dylan up here and left me in

California?"

"You're a grown-up, Glen." Her voice shook, but not with anger: with contempt. "No one *left* you anywhere. You had options. You could still choose to move if you wanted."

"The way I remember it, I wasn't given any options to choose from."

She tugged at the hanks of hair at her temples. "I can't do this anymore. I can't. It's too much."

Glen walked to her and put a hand on her shoulder, but he couldn't bring himself to embrace her. "Janice."

She kept pulling at her hair.

He took a step back and trapped her hands in his.

"How are the physical therapy sessions coming along?"

"Real good!"

There was a sound of a foot scraping on the floor where Dylan and the doctor stood behind them. Glen and Janice dropped their hands. Glen felt like they'd been caught as lovers with their fingers laced together, or two people who care about what happens to one another.

Dylan's face was unreadable.

Dr. Erdogan wore the neutral expression of a medical professional. Too often he came in on the hissed arguments of people caught up in a tragedy and failing to come through the experience intact. The rotund little doctor smiled down at the child and raised his gaze to Dylan's parents. "Dylan's our gold star patient. Your family really has something to celebrate! We can cut back on the checkups if he keeps up with his exercises. Dylan, remember what your therapists told you about the exercise routine?"

"The more I do now, the less I need later," Dylan recited.

"Right." Dr. Erdogan wore the inevitable hospital whites, while Dylan was draped in clothing two sizes too big. He was pale as he stood next to the dark-skinned doctor. But Dylan showed off the new exercises he'd mastered with a confident concentration.

"Watch me do the helicopter!"

Dylan talked to his father and spun his arms, demonstrating the improved range of motion in his left shoulder. Janice and Dr. Erdogan discussed the newest exercises. Their voices emerged from a filter at the far end of a stethoscope. "Blah blah blah," came out of Janice's mouth. "Blah blah blah."

Glen pinched the bridge of his nose, but the sounds stayed meaningless. Only the high clear voice of his son came through. *It's over.* The back of his brain rejoiced as it repeated Dr. Erdogan's statement that Dylan had a clean bill of health. *This whole ordeal is over.*

He made the appropriate responses to what the good doctor had to say, shook hands at the correct juncture, even put an arm around Janice's shoulders as she and he and their child waited for the elevator. When it came they climbed in and began the descent. As he stood dully in the elevator, his son in bright focus as everything else lost meaning, Glen's only feeling was joy.

A Little Boy's Ghost

The months of waiting for Dylan's medical care team to say Dylan would return to childhood were over. But in the long difficult process of getting Dylan on the road to a full recovery, Janice and Glen strayed off their own course. They lost their bearings, and they never got them back.

Glen convinced himself he wouldn't stay bitter about Janice. When she remarried two years later Glen wished her all the luck in the world and he meant the words…. After all, Janice's happiness ensured his son's happiness.

The most painful part, an ache that never left him, was that the end of his marriage meant the end of his family. After the divorce, missing details defined Glen's life. It was the absence of his son's daily mood swings. Dylan's graduation from third and fourth and fifth and sixth grades. The bringing home of tests aced or squeaked by. Sweetly meaningless arguments about whose turn it was to carry the sack of glass jars and bottles out for recycling.

Glen lost the mundane.

A part of Glen's story stopped with Dylan at age eight. The house froze in time, the ghosts of his wife and son moving through the rooms. Janice's ghost faded faster than Glen expected. But in the rooms of Glen's northern California house, his son is eight years old and uninjured. Dylan loves his daddy forever in the present tense.

A larger, taller silhouette grew to fill in the outline of that little boy. Dylan spent every summer with Glen and every vacation, including Christmas.

"You're not even religious!" Janice protested.

Glen remained stubborn. He wasn't going to lose any more days with his child.

After the terrible accident Dylan's wounds healed and became pliable scars. Glen's injuries were psychic. Emotional. They ached no less for being unseen. "Dylan survived," Glen told himself. "Janice and I didn't." Glen didn't know a part of himself hadn't either.

Virtual Realities

At some point in the telling we've moved over to the motel bed. Glen pulls me close and buries his face in my shoulder.

My arms go around him and I hold him with all the compassion I can summon.

When he can talk again, he loosens his hold on me and the past. "That chapter you picked.... You want to escape to the North Pole? Well, Dylan did. He vanished into a video game, he went into a virtual reality called SnowWorld. Dylan used it whenever the hospital staff treated his burns. When this happens burn patients experience the excruciating pain all over again. In SnowWorld he was playing, throwing snowballs at penguins and big woolly mammoths and igloos and snowmen. In the real world," Glen's eyes are shut as he pushes his forehead hard against my breastbone, "they were scraping his wounds. The goal was to make him believe he was interacting with that other world where it was cold, not burning hot. The VR was specially designed for child burn victims."

"Timber! I'm so sorry!" I picture a little boy wearing a helmet and headphones which allow him to escape the pain of necessary hospital procedures. "Talk about going to extremes!"

"As parents we couldn't even agree on his therapy. Janice was scared SnowWorld would make Dylan schizophrenic. An alternate reality to help him get through his pain sounded to me like a *good* thing. I thank God for SnowWorld. Anything was better than having him addicted to opiates. I'm a stunt man, for Christ's sake! I know about creating convincing illusions, and Dylan's hold on the real world is solid. He's more than grounded."

More than Enough

"Janice blamed me for everything. It was my fault for moving us away from San Francisco. And no hospital a mile from the new house. And that I hadn't supervised the kids better. But it was her fault we fought that morning. And she'd *watched* from the window, waiting for me to screw up rather than coming outside to say something or warn me. I'm telling you, we had more than enough recriminations and guilt to pass around."

Glen doggedly goes on. "They stayed in Washington and we put our problems on a back burner. Fine choice of words, huh. By the time we got around to fixing the marriage it was too late. In the end, I understand why she took Dylan to Seattle. But she took my son from me. I will never forgive that." The piercing blue of his eyes remains, their laser directed inward. My old friend is honest, no matter how painful the truths he faces.

"I flew up every chance I could. I couldn't prevent my son from getting burned, and I couldn't stop Janice from taking him away. But I made damned sure we went to counseling. I insisted; remember I told you I'm a control freak? Well, that's when it started. I enjoyed making her face what she was doing by taking our son from his father.

"The divorce was fair. Even control freaks and out-of-control wives have their decent sides. The important thing was, be there for Dylan." Glen clears his throat several times. "They did a skin graft for the big burn on his back. There's the danger of nerve damage and lack of sensation. A scar that deep can end up not pliable." Glen emphasizes the last two words. "I hated the details of what *that* meant. He needed physical therapy. And exercises. And massage to stretch the healing tissues and new layers of skin and prevent them from sticking to the muscles and bones underneath." He shudders. "Nikita, you should've seen him. One of us or one of the therapists worked with him every single day. He never complained, never. Not once. The closest he ever came was to mumble that he was tired and needed a break."

"Well, we know where he gets his stoicism, Timber."

"Me, stoic? I'm the world's biggest pain wimp. Being a stunt man just toughened me up."

"I only mean you accept things without whining." I put a hand under his T-shirt and run my fingers over the souvenirs of his career. A patch of hardened tissue on his left side by his rib cage; a spot on his right shoulder where he'd gotten hit by a flying piece of scenery.

"Doing inventory, lady?"

I trace his smiling lips, oddly relieved he has no facial

scars. For some reason those would be bad, while the ones on his frame are just marks of the trade. But what a shame that his good looks are never recorded. The camera rarely does close-ups of people doing stunts.

His ability to imitate the gait and body language of famous actors make him a good stunt man. It isn't only the ability to take a fall, in all senses of the term; it's to take it for someone else. Like the way Glen absorbed the death of his marriage if it meant his son would be all right. Like the way he's driving me to my husband in Seattle.

What's it like when your child is wrenched from your arms, literally flown out of them by a pilot? I've known Glen most of my life, and our stories have come together to merge as one. His tale feels like it's my own.

The Play of Children

"A Burn Ward.... There's antiseptics, of course, but underneath is a kind of scorched-earth aroma."

"Does Dylan talk about the experience?"

"He says he doesn't remember much of his first week on the ward and I hope that's the truth. The worst part is when they change bandages. Everything's hospital white, and red blood seeps out. It's an awful sight. I can't imagine what it was like for him. Thank God he had SnowWorld. When I saw some of the other patients, I knew we were lucky. Nikita, patients had been in industrial accidents or car crashes, or worse. One guy had basically showered in boiling water –." The story changes direction. "The children on the floor made it all bearable, and unbearable. These sorts of things should never happen to kids.

"The patients passed the time playing cards or board games. That part made it bearable. Kids play and laugh and go on with living. Dylan says everyone was nice to him. He remembers we showed up each day with video games and comic books. He took the comic books, but the only game he wanted to play was SnowWorld. Every Friday Harborview brought in pizza, popcorn and candy for everyone. It was movies night. God bless him, Dylan bragged to everyone about how his daddy was a stunt man. I ended up being part of those Friday features...."

I touch his cheek, and he kisses my palm and holds it there.

"Dylan's scars are where you can't see them. I get down on my knees every day to give thanks those fireworks didn't go off in his face. You can't imagine how cruel people are."

"Yeah I can! Theresa and Danny come home every other week with stories about someone at school being mobbed. And I got teased constantly by you and my brother! We weren't young that long ago, Timber."

He laughs, and the sound is sweet. "You have no idea how much your family meant to me. In my house, every tension stayed right there between my mother and father until the morning she packed up and disappeared. All of a sudden she was – gone. My dad never recovered. I swore there was no way I'd make the mistakes my parents did! But my family fell apart too, from one day to the next. You know, in a weird way history's always looping. Sometimes I think life consists of us going around in circles, trying to make things that happened earlier all right again. Or trying to correct things we did to other people without meaning to." A muscle in his cheek twitches. "Randy took care of everything. He taxied me around, booked my flight, packed my bags."

"Are you driving me to Seattle as a way to repay him?"

Glen rubs his head back and forth against my breasts. "Randy and I don't keep score. We were best friends from our first snow ball fight. And now there's you." He stops, then finishes the statement. "You guys are part of my life, that's just how it is. I'm not fatalistic. But our destinies keep crossing paths."

Friday

Mapping my Marital Discord

I surprise myself with matching candor. "Rich and I had Louie to recommit. As a second chance."

"Did it work?"

I stare at the faded photographs of the California coastline on the walls. "Not really. You know the scenario; it didn't do anything for the marriage, but we have two great daughters and this amazing boy."

Theresa, named for my mom, is the spitting image of me at that age: poised with plenty of self-confidence. Danny is a Daniella. We named her for Rich's father Daniel. When I was pregnant with Danny the task of holding together as a couple, much less as a family of four, seemed more than we could manage.

The marriage smoothed out, or I grew used to its ragged borders. Later, years later, we tried for a son.

Rich couldn't understand why this was important to me. "Isn't my testosterone enough for three, babe?" he teased.

Rich loves kids and couldn't care less if they're boys or girls. But I want the energy a boy provides. I need my daughters to know how to live with a young man in the same house. Their father's horseplay isn't the same thing. I can't explain it or if I tried, Rich didn't listen.

Rich had wanted a big family. But Louie's such a hyperactive little boy that he conceded three children were enough. Louis is intense! He combines my energy with his father's New York intensity. In a seven-year-old, this combination means *I want* and *I need* are imperatives, not requests.

I hear Louie's demanding voice calling out to me where I lie beside Glen on a motel bed with a yellow spread, and my candor evaporates. I don't want to talk about how I feel.

Instead, I offer, "You know what Louie kept asking?"

Fly Me Like an Airplane

"Mommy! Why aren't you coming with us?"

"Daddy needs to prove he's master of the wilderness."

Rich placed his palms over Louie's ears. "Don't listen to Mommy, she's jealous she isn't coming along to revive her Girl Scout credentials!" My husband laughed uproariously and headed outdoors to mow the lawn.

"But *why*?" Louie ran to the couch where I sat filling out the conference registration forms. He threw himself on top of me.

"Oof!"

He hugged me hard, refusing to let my head go as he tugged my hair. "*I'll miss you*," he informed me.

I moved the paperwork away. "Mommy will miss you. You know what?" I told my fellow chocoholic, "I'll bring you back chocolates from Ghirardelli Square."

"I want you to come with *us*! I don't *want* chocolates." For the first time, my son refused the offer of sweets. "You always come when we go somewhere," Louie accused. His hold around my head tightened as he hugged harder.

I pulled Louie into my lap and held him in place with a hug of my own. "Honey, why are you so upset?"

"It's for all of three weeks, Louie." Theresa sat in Rich's easy chair painting her toenails a lurid orange. "And Dad takes cool detours," she reminded her brother.

I snorted. "Detours? You mean, he has a lousy sense of direction, refuses to follow the map, and no one says anything when he takes a wrong turn."

"We see new stuff when Dad drives." Theresa finished her nails and sat back. Dark hair hung heavy around her shoulders. She pushed it out of her face with one hand and worked the cap back onto the polish with the other.

As I looked at her I became aware of her clothing, or lack of them. "Theresa, since when do stores sell shirt halves?"

Friday

She checked her toes and examined her bare midriff; she was the picture of calm. "Hang on a minute." When Theresa was satisfied the nails were dry, she got to her feet and left the living room.

Five minutes later she was back with an old photo album. She pursed her lips in a parody of sternness as she flipped pages. "Why am I not allowed at almost seventeen to wear a shirt that shows my belly button, when you wore clothes ten times worse?"

My daughter tapped her finger on a photograph of me as a teenager. My tight green shirt's puckered material left nothing to the imagination about the shape or fullness of my breasts. In the photo I wore more makeup than Theresa ever dares to, at least before she leaves the house.

I gave her a weak smile and thought, *At least her shirt doesn't cling.* "Please don't get any tattoos or body piercings while you're out tonight."

"Yes!" Theresa pumped a triumphant fist in the air. She vacated the house before I could change my mind.

"Ten o'clock!" I called after her. "It's a school night!"

Her sister sat on the rug, petting Taffy as the purring cat lay across her legs. "How come she gets to wear what she wants and I can't?"

"You're fourteen, Danny. You know the rules." This time I'm firm. I can't let all three children manipulate me in the same evening. As a mother I have my pride.

Louie had wriggled out of my embrace while I argued with Theresa. He went in the kitchen and stood in front of the refrigerator.

"No chips!" I called.

He got out the juice.

Danny set Taffy aside and came to the couch to claim her brother's place. Petulant, she seated herself beside me. I stroked her soft blond hair and she leaned back, her frame still pencil-thin. I smiled, glad she couldn't see my face. I keep a soft spot for Daniella. Danny isn't mature like her cheeky, popular sister and she's far less demanding than her brother.

"Honey, you just turned fourteen. You'll grow up soon enough." I didn't want to tell her about the treacherous gaps that remained to be breached. "I'm not ready to lose my littlest girl yet." It's true; I'm terribly unprepared for the moment each child declares independence. Admitting that Theresa had turned into a young woman was hard. She'd grown up overnight when my attention was elsewhere.

Danny retrieved a brush from under the couch cushions before yielding back into my embrace. "Do my hair?"

"So that's where my brush disappeared to!" I took the tool in my hands and brushed.

"Daddy says not to tell you he'll need our help setting up the tent and cooking on the camp stove. He's afraid he's going to make a dumb mistake again and you'll find out and get mad," she confided.

I wasn't sure whether to laugh or cry at the information. It wasn't like my husband to enlist our children's help. And to admit he was worried he'd blow it and reap my disdain... this new element to our difficult dynamics twisted inside me like shrapnel.

The front door banged and Rich came in with his arms folded, pretending outrage. "Is it true you gave Theresa permission to leave the house with half her shirt gone?"

"Maybe it shrank in the wash?" I shrugged, still holding the brush.

"Next thing we know she'll run off to join the circus." He fixed his gaze on Danny and narrowed his eyes. Rich glowered and pointed a finger. "And as for you...."

She squirmed, giggling.

"*You*, young lady, I'm sending to a convent. No dates till I'm dead, and I plan to live to one hundred and forty."

Louie came up behind his father and tackled him at the knees with a body slam. "What about me?"

Rich winked at me and Danny. Without missing a beat, he flipped Louie over his head and lowered him to the rug. "It's the Louis Gleason secret password: 'What about *me*?' Used any time you feel left out of a discussion." Rich grabbed Louie by the ankles and swung him around in front of the sofa. Danny's little brother whistled back and forth through the air. "*You*, sir, will join the Foreign Legion. You'll go live in a fort in the desert. It'll build *character*." Rich winked again, including us in the conspiracy.

"No. I. Won't." Louie stretched his arms out in delight, making his body a projectile. His hair waved, his cheeks turning red as blood rushed down into his face. "No. I. Won't!"

Danny jumped off the couch. "Swing me. Play airplane with me, too." Her voice was a little girl's. "Please? Come on, Daddy. Fly me like an airplane."

Rich tossed Louie, still protesting happily, onto the couch beside me. Danny plopped on the floor by her father's feet. Rich reached down and grasped her left hand and ankle. "The things I do for my kids." Rich groaned loudly, as if Daniella weighed three hundred pounds instead of one hundred and five. "When did you get so heavy, Danny-o?"

Louie threw himself across the couch onto me. Shrieking, the two of us collapsed into a pile on the pillows.

An American Film

I wind up my recital and feel forlorn. Resentment bubbles up whenever I mention Rich. My family images, though, are idyllic. I don't relive the difficult days; what I feel is a shiver of what Glen described when he lost Dylan.

What I feel is a piece of me has ripped from my body and gone missing. *Focus on getting to my kids. I can think about everything else later.*

"Nikita: Doyenne of Domesticity... what are you

thinking?"

"How intensely I miss them." Sadness drives through me like a lance. "Timber," I groan.

"It's your call," he says quietly. "I'm free and clear in all the ways that matter." It's true. Glen's emotions for me aren't conflicted. He doesn't want me to suffer, but he isn't going to make the choices easy for me. He feels the pressure, too. Time's running out.

We embrace tightly. A motel room is terrible; it is impersonal; it is a refuge. The sanctuary it offers isn't ever enough, because it's temporary. Like a cockpit instrument, the clock in the room continues the inexorable recording of lapsed time and growing pressures.

"I can't think! There isn't any time to think! Everything happened so fast. I can't think," I keep repeating. My throat hurts as words force themselves up and out. "It's so complicated because of falling in love."

Glen's eyes flicker for a split second as I declare my feelings for the first time. He strokes my torso, but my inner tension refuses consolation.

"The cyberattacks hit and it seemed like the world was ending so I slept with you, and then I couldn't fly away and I don't *want* to fly away, but I need to meet Rich in three days and my God I want my kids. Timber, I'm scared! I don't know what we've found but whatever it is we're already losing it!"

He kisses me. "You know what," he offers, "I've realized I want this to be a film. An American one. You know: totally illogical. The heroes rush in and save the day. Tragedy is averted and danger is defused at the last minute. No one gets hurt. But bad things did happen. People got hurt," his soft, self-ironic tone confides. "People even got killed. This is no film. It's a nightmare, with one major difference. You. You being here changes everything. I never imagined I could feel so horrified and happy both at the same time."

It's true. Glen radiates the joy only a mature man with deep grief in his past is capable of transmitting. Anyone who loves like he loves Dylan is a full human being. I may be the cause of this masculine joy, but I'm also the grateful and needy recipient.

Glen holds me close and I'm enveloped in his glow and it's okay for him to love me. Opened up to love, I realize how much I need it.

The Bottom Line

Later I lie and savor how he breathes in and out, in and out. I'm grateful he's in the bed. Sex or no sex, I don't want to be alone.

I can't sleep. Out of nowhere an image swims up: the last office function I attended.

At the end of the year Rich's company had a holiday party. It was quiet that day at the animal shelter and I left early. People hadn't yet started bringing in the unwanted animals received as holiday gifts.

The offices were still decorated. Garlands hung over the company logo. Lights reflected off strands of silver and gold glitter a secretary had draped on a Christmas tree in careful rows. Somewhere on the floor people were singing an off-color version of *Deck the Halls*.

I checked Rich's office, but it was locked. Miranda, the department manager, sat at her desk. She bent over, tugging at the stockings she wore under a plaid winter dress.

"You made it!" Miranda recovered quickly. "Hi, Nicole. Rich wasn't sure if you'd be coming." Her tone was stiff, but Miranda and I had never hit it off.

"Is he around?"

"Everyone just headed for the conference room."

"Thanks, Miranda." I walked away before she could pretend to engage me in friendly conversation.

The conference room was filled with staff and their significant others, helping themselves to catered food. A fragrant spray of jonquils scented the air. Liquor bottles lined one end of the table.

I spotted my husband standing with the sales reps. All were twenty pounds' overweight and hungry for a deal. All carried cell phones; they formed an electronic posse at the OK Corral.

Rich waved an arm, his face flushed. "Someone told me a new one yesterday."

I'd been about to make my presence known, but my husband tells a great joke.

"One fine weekend in August, Sherlock Holmes and Doctor Watson went camping," Rich began. "They found a clearing in a remote spot in the woods. The two set up a tent and fell asleep. Some hours later, Holmes woke his faithful friend. 'Watson,' Sherlock Holmes spoke urgently. 'Look up at the sky and describe what you see.'

"Watson obediently stared up into the skies. 'I see millions of stars.'

"'What do they tell you?' Holmes asked.

"As usual, his companion was setting a puzzle to be solved. Watson pondered. 'Their light tells me there are millions of suns and galaxies beyond what I can count. According to the constellations, Jupiter is in Leo. The warm air and the trees' full foliage indicate late summer. From where the moon is over there on the horizon, time-wise it's a quarter to three. I can see the Milky Way. It follows that tomorrow will be a beautiful day without clouds or rain. We're in the middle of the wilderness, so it's evident we are small and insignificant but safe in the Lord's hands. What do the stars tell you, Holmes?'

"The great detective sighed. 'Watson, you fool, someone's stolen our tent.'"

The conference room burst into laughter.

Friday

"That one's for my wife, who swears I shouldn't be allowed anywhere *near* a camp site," Rich began.

I stepped forward.

"Hey! Speak of the devil and Old Nick arrives! When did *you* get here?" My husband put an arm around me and gave me a kiss. It was more than just a display of good will for his colleagues. "Look at you!" he exclaimed.

I wore a brocade jacket over a white blouse and narrow black skirt. "I changed before I left the shelter."

"Babe, you look *great*. I always tell you, you should dress in skirts more often."

I opened my mouth to retort that I do wear them, as often as time and place allow.

He grew silent, and redder.

I walked to the window where slow traffic crawled along the streets outside. Gray snow sprayed from under tires, sludge like my attempt at holiday enthusiasm. We'd had a short thaw, but then the softened snow turned to dangerous black ice.

"Can I get you something?" Rich asked. How many drinks had he had? Later we planned to head to my parents' house for a family get-together. His hand touched my elbow. "Babe...."

I gave him a smile and pretended I didn't see his guilty expression. "Maybe a cocktail for the spousal unit?"

"Alcohol?"

I nodded, and Rich's face smoothed out as he realized I was passing on righteous indignation.

"I was going to ask if you wanted a gin and tonic," he lied. "Here – take mine."

"If you can't beat'em, join'em!" I brought the glass to my lips to drink, swallowed – and almost choked. It was a double, no, it tasted like a triple. I finished off the drink and followed Rich over to the conference table. He mixed new drinks as he kept up a line of patter.

"How about another?"

"Wonders never cease." Rich grinned and refilled my glass.

I sipped cautiously.

Marty Fuller worked his way around the table to where I stood. He wore a cashmere sweater over gray slacks that exactly matched his graying hair. "Nicole! You made it!" He grasped my hand in an unfeigned welcome. Marty turned to my husband. "Like I asked last week: when are you coming back to us?"

"Never!" Rich answered. "Life takes place outside the office. It's good to get out and see what the competition's up to."

Marty took my glass before I could protest. "Allow me to top off your drink." He replenished his own too, and handed mine back with a smile.

"Nicole!" someone exclaimed, and I turned to say hello to Rich's colleagues. Voices murmured. Should I measure the drinks by the alcohol content or the number of glasses? The room was too warm.

Marty was back. It dawned on me that my husband's boss was flirting. The concept of Marty making a pass at me was absurd... so absurd I smiled back.

Through the open door of the conference room, the lights on the lobby's Christmas tree twinkled. Miranda stood by the window talking with a man. He turned, and it was Rich. My husband bent his head as he listened to what she was earnestly saying.

Marty repeated my name.

"I'm sorry, what did you say?"

"I said, it's nice to see you again. Rich tells me the shelter keeps you busy and that's why you don't come to many office functions. Do you have a *lot* of women staying there?"

"Women?" I was baffled. "Oh! I get it, you're thinking of a women's shelter!" I began to laugh and couldn't stop.

Friday

"Yeah, women and children and house pets. All those helpless creatures. No, no, no." My head felt thick.

Marty observed me with concern.

"I run an an-nim-mal shelter," I enunciated.

"Oh Christ! I knew that," said Marty. "I feel like an idiot."

I touched his hand with mine. "It's okay."

"You just don't look like someone who works with strays," he added, and his direct look swam through my fuzzy vision to embrace my outfit. His fingers squeezed.

"Well," I remarked. I braced my free palm against the conference table.

He put an arm around me. "Dizzy?"

"Don't tell me, the drink was a triple."

In the other room Rich shook his head again at Miranda. She put out a hand and he grasped her wrist, stopping her movement. Miranda's arm dropped to her side and Rich turned. He crossed the lobby and came back in the conference room to where I leaned against mahogany.

Marty's hold tightened as Rich came closer. My husband's boss gave me a hug. "You're a lucky bastard, Rich." Reluctantly Marty removed the arm. "That last drink I made Nicole was a little strong."

"You know holiday parties," Rich agreed. "Everyone likes them strong, and Nicole can't drink to begin with."

"I need to get something in my stomach." I turned to find silverware. I got a plate of food and sat down; I couldn't eat fast enough. When my plate was empty I rejoined them.

"Feeling better?" Rich asked.

"Ready for another?" Marty asked, before Rich could do the chivalrous honors. Marty mixed me a fresh gin and tonic. I took the proffered drink. "A toast to the coming year!"

"Here, here!" we approved, and lifted our glasses.

A young woman held up a bunch of bright berries with silvery green leaves. "Time for mistletoe!"

I shook my head back and forth, trying to focus. Suddenly, I was furious. "*Rich.*" I pulled him over to a corner. I stared over the rim of my drink. "Would you say that you're a glorified ambulance chaser?"

"What? God no, of course not! *Everyone* needs insurance."

I grasped his arm. "What's *your* insurance?"

Rich looked at me sharply.

"I'm not trying to pick a fight. I really want to know."

He gave me another sharp look and drained his drink. "You and the kids, Nick. The four of you are all that stand between me and the void. You don't get that? That's *what it is* for any man with a family. I've told you a hundred times: the job's a game. A game," he repeated quietly. "I do it for what isn't a game: you."

My husband sounded out of character and I didn't like how serious he was. "Let me read the fine print." I wiggled my eyebrows at him.

"Nick, let's get out of here. We still have to get the kids and go to your folks'."

"Oh come on." I patted his solid butt. "Show me your holiday policy's bottom line," I giggled.

Rich rolled his eyes as he hugged me. "I love you when you try to drink. You'll regret this later, but not before I take advantage of you! By the way, I think Marty hopes you'll grant him sexual favors."

"It *would* be a big favor!"

Rich laughed and hugged me closer. "Did I ever tell you the one about how the woman boss chose which applicant to hire?"

We headed out the door, laughing. I caught a glimpse of Miranda's face: it wore a desperate tenderness. She saw me watching and held my eyes. Miranda stared at us (at Rich) and raised her hands to her temples, massaging them. Her gaze dropped as she went red. I wondered, looking at her expression, if she had a migraine.

SATURDAY

Tag. I'm It.

I'm silent for the first hour north of Eureka.

"You want the radio? Maybe we can pick up news somewhere," Glen suggests.

"Later." I can't stop thinking about that office party.

I place myself back in the appreciative audience listening to my husband tell his joke. I relive the way he refreshed drinks and made sure everyone enjoyed themselves. I witness again his intimacy with the office manager, *Miranda, her name is Miranda*. I force myself to name the problem.

I reconsider Miranda's artificial friendliness and her hollow questions about how I and the children are. No wonder she's always strained when I call or come in. She's in love with Rich, or she lusts after him.

My husband, the self-described man of action, is happiest using his aggressive masculinity to get things done. And those *things* are nothing less than the well-being of everyone for whom he feels responsible.

Rich is a caretaker. He cajoles Theresa and Danny and Louie out of their sulks. He provides insurance policies to protect companies and their employees. Rich is solicitous of his coworkers, and that category *definitely* includes Miranda.

Rich is a caretaker. Yes. How have I never seen this before?

I'm discomfited by the memory of Rich's last words. He'd never spoken those words aloud before. "I do it for what isn't a game: you."

Tag. I'm it. If it's a game, I've been calling it by the wrong name.

All I can think is, *Rich should get to adore and be adored, like everyone else gets to. He's more than the sum of his job. He's so much more.*

I see again the longing on Miranda's face as Rich and I left the office party. Her passion for him had shown, intense and present, before she swiftly hid it.

I'm jealous. Yes, jealous! Images flood my understanding in a picture show of glimpsed body language. I turn memories over and over, trying for once to understand a thing by relying on intuition.

My God, Rich is having an affair with Miranda. Maybe for years; maybe it's just beginning. Maybe that's why he went into Sales. Business trips mean hotel rooms. I know myself what those mean....

I Would Not Wish any Companion in the World but You

South of Crescent City we drive through more of the giant trees I've fallen in love with. The sight of the Redwoods National Park distresses me. This world isn't capable of sustaining those magnificent sentinels.

We cross the Oregon border. "How about we switch places? You've been doing all the driving." Those are my first words since we left the redwoods.

Glen pulls to the side of the road. I open the car door and the sound of the surf floods my ears. Its dull roar drowns my confusion but underscores what seethes in my limbs. I run ahead, to leave behind Glen and the wreckage of the world and our sorry histories.

I reach the beach and rip off my sandals. When I splash in the water I gasp. The surf is colder than I expect, colder than California. The world's shifting. There's nothing to stop the next group of hackers from doing a whole lot more damage. Whatever made me think I was safe and my version of reality free from danger?

"Nikita!"

I'm gasping, and not from the unexpected tonic of cold water. I shut my eyes tight and put a hand to my mouth. I bite down and taste salt that might be the ocean.

Glen splashes after me. "Nikita! Ni*cole*." His fingers close on my shoulder and he turns me.

I face the continent behind him. I picture what maybe lies wrecked on both sides of the ocean.

"It's okay, whatever it is. You can tell me. It's okay." His face is grave.

It's not that I want comforting – okay, maybe I do. I kiss him to keep from saying his name back, from the word *Glen* pronounced aloud. It might reveal too much: *I am so frightened. I can't fly away.* It would add, *but this is why I've fallen in love with you.* Further, *I'm glad you stand here at my side. Except for my children, I would not wish any companion in the world but you.*

"I don't want to love you!" I say instead, and mean the same thing.

Losing the Trail

I'm disgusted. The situation requires my self-control, not self-indulgence. The world is in chaos and I've taken a lover while trying to get to my husband. I'm not being rational and I don't know how to feel. I don't know *what* to feel. And maybe rational isn't enough anymore, and that possibility terrifies me....

I'm doing everything in my power to reach Seattle. As if that makes things better. As if it brings back the world before my affair and Rich's affair and the vanished time before we grew apart and our marriage unraveled.

I don't know if I hope that he's heard the news, or remains camped out somewhere far from civilization. They're in the Canyonlands or Zion National Park, someplace before he herds the kids into the minivan to drive the final distance to Seattle. Or maybe they already reached Washington and are somewhere on the Olympic Peninsula. Who knows? I'm frantic and angry, but I shock myself by laughing.

It's not my complicated guilt at my lack of guilt.

It's not the horror of the current world crisis.

It's not the irony that I discovered my husband's having an affair only because I began one of my own.

No, my main worry is Ranger Danger will stray off a marked trail and get hurt.

Implants and Intuition

We go back to the BMW and get out the picnic. I try to reach my family; Rich's cell phone remains silent.

We walk down the beach. Glen drapes the car blanket over a wide driftwood log, and we perch on it facing the ocean. I dig my feet into warm sand and pretend the heat can reach my chilled heart.

It's almost high tide and the beach is a narrow strip. People pass within a few feet of where we sit and eat our picnic meal. It's surreal, a pleasant coastal spot with people tossing Frisbees, building sand castles, walking their dogs. And talking about how the largest hacker attack in history had broken into NSA computers.

"It's ironic. The hackers used NSA plans!"

"How do you mean?"

"Spyware orders implanted on our cell phones and computers to deliver detailed information about what we do. Us, companies, governments... something like 70,000 spy implants around the world. They function like terrorist sleeper cells and can be activated with a mouse click. They attacked Internet routers, everything. Banking systems shut down and markets crashed."

"Everything Snowdown predicted came true...."

Glen deliberately introduces a different subject as he passes me a sandwich half. "Dylan's a great human being. I admire him."

I bite into roast beef. "I've always thought our characters get decided from the time we're babies. In the womb, even. My three kids never cease to amaze me. Their personalities are so different."

"Kids develop depending on environment. Dylan became sensitive from having to gauge what was going on with me and Janice at any given time. Man, being an only child sucks!"

"You're an only child, and you're good with people."

"Just certain people. Not having siblings gave me the desire to dive in a good film the way some people dive into books. Child of my generation, I was. Dylan, though…. He could always make friends. When we moved to Marin, he approached other kids to get included in the games. He introduced himself, asked questions like, 'Which house do you live in? We just moved into the green house two blocks *that* way.'"

Down the beach, a small yellow dragon dips and flutters on a string in the weak wind.

"Did the accident change him?"

"When he got out of the hospital Dylan was more tender. Not like he'd reverted to being a younger child, but somehow he became gentle. Intuitive, even. He could always tell how we were doing. Janice and I sat him down and explained we weren't splitting up because of him. He listened without saying a word. Ten minutes later he returned with his latest exercise report from the therapists, about how well he was doing. He was consoling *us*, instead of the other way around."

Glen digs a foot in the sand, his sandwich forgotten. "He's surprisingly well adjusted. He went out for basketball because he's a tall kid. He plays the trumpet and says he'll keep up with lessons this year. I'm pretty sure he doesn't get hassled about his scars." Glen smooths a palm over the surface of the driftwood. "He's lived in Seattle long enough for it to feel like home. That's the advantage of moving to an area with a good economy. Everyone's from somewhere else."

"Unlike Grovesville, where our parents all grew up or moved there as young married couples. *We* got to inherit whatever the town decided about them," I contribute. "It sounds as if Dylan's a little like the way I am with animals, but he can do it with people."

"He has an affinity for any inarticulate life form that can't express itself. Which is ninety-nine percent of human beings ninety-nine percent of the time." Glen smiles to take the sting of cynicism from his words. He stands. "Come on, Nikita: Queen of Sweets. We need to get to the next town."

When we reach the car I take the wheel. "Read to me?"

He opens the book. "I already know what country I'm picking. India."

Goa was Portuguese

"Another warm Goa morning. The heat wasn't oppressive… yet. Kim sat at one end of the breakfast table in a striped cotton skirt and white T-shirt. She was touring India in April just ahead of the monsoon season, and the weather was far more humid than she'd anticipated. She drank tea and tried to write postcards.

Kim was the one solo traveler on the tour, but she was in good company. The group was small. Greg and Beth hailed from Lincoln, Nebraska, and Leigh and Harry came from Berkeley. All four were well-heeled professionals, freshly retired. They'd bonded with Kim, amused to find themselves in India with fellow Americans.

Traveling with them were two frivolous Australian friends, Gavin and Ross, and a young couple from Holland. Jan and Anna explained they were splurging on the tour to stay in places with working showers. Their clothes hung loose on their bodies They'd suffered bouts of Delhi belly in their three months of taking public trains and busses across India. Kim felt sympathy for the Dutch pair, rather than sneering that they should travel less on the cheap – or be more careful about what they ate.

The Australians were literally coming down from a trek and kept up a patter of jokes. "Bed bugs, incredible old forts and palaces, the shits, elephant rides, Arjuna Cave, India has it all!" Gavin exclaimed.

"Don't listen to him, he's still high from the trek. Or maybe what he smoked back on the beach during the full moon rave." Ross pulled his sun bleached locks back into a pony tail.

Her pen hovered as Kim considered. "You guys, what should I write?"

"Goa belonged to Portugal until 1961," Leigh offered.

"Velha Goa was a vast trading empire, with a city of over two hundred thousand people before plagues hit in the eighteenth century. The survivors fled, the city's stayed deserted and empty ever since," Harry read over his wife's shoulder from her guide book.

"Old Goa's bloody huge and bloody sterile," Ross stated.

"We haven't toured the cathedral yet," Gavin reminded him.

Ross rolled his eyes. "A saint missing an arm. Oh, joy."

The Reluctant Pilgrim

Kim wandered around the giant gilded basilica, so carefully tended. She thought, *This entire city's a mausoleum.* The site was as preserved as the one-armed remains of St. Francis Xavier.

Old Goa was once the center for evangelizing the Far East. Francis Xavier had destroyed Goa's ancient temples and sent missives begging Rome to bring on the Inquisition. He died in 1552 on a mission to convert China, and two years later his corpse was sent back to Goa. Francis Xavier's body hadn't decayed. It was a miracle! In 1614, his baptizing right forearm was chopped off and sent to Rome as proof of his saintly, incorruptible state.

When Kim had told her friends back home about the tour, everyone was excited. "Wow! India! You'll have incredible adventures! It has the most powerful spiritual energy. They say you go to India and come back changed."

She'd responded with vague remarks; Kim was a reluctant pilgrim. She didn't trust people who talked about India as a portal to enlightenment.

Goa was too Western for her tastes after all. After ten days on the beach, she hungered for the real India... whatever that was. She wouldn't experience more than a small chunk of the subcontinent. What did she expect, beach parties or yoga in ashrams? Goat curry, or moguls and the Taj Mahal? Ayurveda medicine, or Kashmir shawls? Nonviolent resistance, or gang rape and murder on a public bus? Castes and slums and hovels, or India's headlong advances as a BRIC nation?

There was surely more than the mutilated saint of Goa's Catholicism. "There are as many religions as there are people on the planet," Gandhi had said. India was Hindu and as easily Muslim and Buddhist and Zoroastrian and Christian and Jain and Sikh and Baha'i and....

And, Kim reminded herself, *India's a mirror. Travelers who expect poverty and squalor find both in spades. Visitors seeking enlightenment find that, too. What am I here for? If I stay open minded, what'll I find?* She chewed the tip of her pen. *Goa was Portuguese,* she considered writing, *and gorgeous ocean views, the rave scene and meals eaten in beach shacks.* Every sentence sounded like factoids from a travelogue.

Kim put away her postcards unfinished.

Holy Cows

They faced a long drive to the neighboring state of Karnataka. The tour office had assigned them a guide. Nupur

Saturday

was a tiny woman of four foot eleven inches and shining, thick black hair. Nupur wore a red dot between her brows and her sari like the robes of a queen.

Their minivan came with a driver and his son. Each time they reached a bad place on the dirt roads the small boy jumped out to assess it. Kim saw deep potholes and was glad for their combined care.

The sun beat down. They drove through parched countryside that needed the rain the monsoons would bring. Each home they passed had water sprinkled in the dirt before the door to keep down dust.

Finally, they reached Hampi, and Hampi looked nothing like the beaches of Goa. Hampi was a desert. The landscape consisted of huge sandstone boulders with the Tungabhadra River running through it. Here the Hindu god Shiva was the consort of Pampa, goddess of the river.

When they saw where the bus was heading, everyone gasped.

"Holy cow! Look at the tower!" Greg exclaimed.

The Virupaksha temple was a pyramid topped with a spire and a red flag. Impressive from a distance, up close the temple was gargantuan. It towered a hundred and fifty feet above their heads.

Architects had carved the creamy white stone into decorative levels. Exotic gods. Strange goddesses. Female figures spraddle-legged and touching themselves.

A gigantic wooden chariot was parked in the temple's huge courtyard. Long yellow garlands draped the wagon. The top of the chariot hid under a multi-colored cloth. It ballooned out in wide stripes of reds, yellows, oranges and blues. High up, carved lions raised their paws and carved horses reared.

"Tonight this chariot will carry the god Shiva to the river for the Nandi Purnima," Nupur informed them. "It's a Nandi full moon. Nandi's the bull who attends Shiva, so this is extra auspicious."

The tour group left the minivan and gawked, mouths open.

They entered the temple and it was packed with worshippers. The vast interior had high ceilings and numerous alcoves. Incense, dust, and dim light met and mixed.

Little beaks pecked Kim's elbow. "Look at my hands!" demanded a high voice.

Kim looked down and almost fainted. The beggar girl's digits were so grotesquely bent back that they no longer resembled fingers. More cripples crowded towards her, blocking the floor. A boy crawled on all fours with splayed elbows and knees, his hips sticking out at wrong angles. He was maybe ten years old, although with malnutrition he was probably older. "Please, a few coins. A few coins, for food."

Kim didn't want to open her wallet in the crowded, disorienting space. "Maybe later," she stalled. She hurried after the others.

Nupur led them up a short flight of stone stairs. They filed into a narrow hallway that dead ended in a stone wall. A window high above shed dim light. Weak illumination came from a slit in the wall.

Glad I'm not claustrophobic! Kim thought. She could just see the high temple tower through the slit.

A skinny man stood and waved everyone to the sides of the corridor. His hand moved up and down before the slit. An image of the tower appeared on the back wall, first in white and next in shadow. The tower was upright, but in the next instant turned upside down. His brown palm swept up and down and the image flipped accordingly.

Kim made herself concentrate on the dazzling tower she could make it through the slit. Now white, now black. It kept vanishing as the hand moved past. She grew dizzy.

"The architects were experimenting with pinpoint

perspective." Nupur led them down the steps and towards the back of the temple.

"Moo," Kim muttered, but no one was there to share the private snicker at tour groups as they trail a white flag or furled umbrella. She hurried to keep up.

They stepped out into a yard where bricks tumbled on themselves around the remains of a large pool. "For centuries this pool held drinking water. Hindus purified themselves before entering the temple. Since the beginning of time we've used water for sacred rituals." Nupur's voice carried. "Pagans threw coins into streams and springs as offerings to the gods in the depths. Catholics cross themselves with a hand dipped in a font of holy water. Muslims wash their hands and feet before entering the mosque. Jews submerge themselves in temple baths."

It was surprisingly quiet behind the temple. Kim took the opportunity to dig some rupee coins out from the bottom of her purse and contemplate sacred water in a parched yard.

They re-entered the temple and the brief pause outdoors had cleared her sight. Kim could identify groups of pilgrims, chatting and sitting. Believers prayed up on a platform at the main altar. A small boy swung back and forth on the clanging, heavy metal chain hanging in front of the inner sanctum.

The waiting beggars moved forward. Kim gave a crippled boy a coin and tried not to see the others. A bony old priest held out a palm. Paint streaks on his face matched the white of his wispy beard. Kim gave him a coin and pressed her palms together. She stepped around the reaching hands that ended in bird beaks and moved in the direction of the front doors. Nupur and the others had vanished.

Bazaar/Bizarre

Kim's view was simultaneously filled and obstructed. The

front courtyard and Hampi Bazaar Road were crammed with bodies. Worshippers raised their arms to touch Shiva's massive chariot. Mandapams, porch-like structures once used for commerce or the homes of wealthy traders, lined the sides of the street. Pilgrims claimed spots in them, trying to find shade.

Women in brilliant saris walked past. Old crones with henna-patterned arms carried small children. Turbaned men sampled fruit from a pyramid of dates. An all-white cow rested serenely on a pile of garbage. A painted bus had parked in the dust; a pilgrim dozed on one of the seats with his bare feet sticking out through the open window.

Kim peeked in a shop selling cheap clothes and plastic sunglasses. When she turned, she banged her head on a string of water bottles hanging in the doorway. Sunlight reflected off the mirrored insets of embroidered bags and shirts in the next little shop.

She pushed on through the crowds, trying to spot her group. A couple in a patch of shade looked up as she walked past. Their oxen leant against the cool stones of an ancient wall. The bovine pair had their forelegs tucked under them. Their curved horns were painted crimson and capped in metal. Magenta pompoms with orange and blue tassels hung from the tips; a pile of cow shit steamed.

In the middle of the road a clump of pilgrims whispered among themselves, pointing. A man crouched in the dirt. He was perhaps thirty years old, mustachioed and handsome. Thick hair brushed across the white bands smeared on his forehead. He wore a peach-orange cotton shirt and pants. The man knelt, barefoot, on all fours on a rug. A big copper pot dappled with white streaks and red dots balanced on his shoulders. A string of beads wound around the pot's lip. A long cobra slid clockwise over the beads, flicking an orange tongue. Hands darted out from the crowd to touch the snake and drop coins into the pot.

Saturday

Bang! Bang! Bang! Bang! Bang! Bang! Bang! Bang! Bang! Bang! Bang! Bang!

Kim forgot the snake handler and the crowds.

Bang! Bang! Bang! Bang! Bang! Bang! Bang! Bang! Bang! Bang! Bang! Bang!

She forgot the coiling cobra.

Bang! Bang! Bang! Bang! Bang! Bang! Bang! Bang! Bang! Bang! Bang! Bang!

Men banging small metal drums swirled. The noise came nearer and four of them spun, or five, or maybe six. They moved too fast to count. Their faces were bright red. Dreadlocks had been piled up and tied into topknots on their heads.

Bang! Bang! Bang! Bang! Bang! Bang! Bang! Bang! Bang! Bang! Bang! Bang!

Their circle engulfed Kim. She was surrounded by constant movement, constant noise, terrible painted faces moving in and out and around.

Two wildly gesticulating figures neared her in the center of the circle. Like the others, their unkempt hair swung from topknots and they had red faces.

The musicians kept up a steady Bang! Bang! Bang! Bang! Bang! Bang! Bang! Bang! Bang! Bang! Bang! Bang! Something about the dancers was wrong. Kim tried to focus on the figure whirling closest.

He locked his eyes on hers and light glinted off the long knife piercing his cheeks.

Bang! Bang! Bang! Bang! Bang! Bang! Bang! Bang! Bang! Bang! Bang! Bang!

A curving scimitar had been pushed through his flesh to the center of the blade. The knife was at least six inches long. Kim threw a wild glance at the next swirling figure. He had a knife impaled in his face, too.

Bang! Bang! Bang! Bang! Bang! Bang! Bang! Bang! Bang! Bang! Bang! Bang!

Harsh lights flashed off the thick blades. The figures stared wide-eyed as they danced. A drummer thrust out a brown palm.

Kim pointed to her camera and turned away. "I didn't take a picture."

Bang! Bang! Bang! Bang! Bang! Bang! Bang! Bang! Bang! Bang! Bang! Bang!

The circle remained and somehow the drummer reappeared in front of her. He placed a flat palm, insistent and implacable, against her breastbone. He wouldn't allow her to step away.

All Kim wanted was to escape the eyes in those red faces.

Bang! Bang! Bang! Bang! Bang! Bang! Bang! Bang! Bang! Bang! Bang! Bang!

She grabbed a coin out of her pocket. The coin changed palms and somewhere up high in the air behind Kim came a hard inhuman laugh. Without pity it acknowledged her terror and her alms. The drummer stepped away, the dancers swirled.

Then they vanished. Thousands of Indians blocked the dirt road once again, and the dreams of maya continued in their splendor.

She found the others at last, resting in a mandapam as they waited for her. They worked through the crowds back to their minivan. The group chatted as they waited for the driver and his son to return.

As dusk arrived men in yellow robes sat cross-legged on the ground by huge colored stones, calmly gazing off in the direction of the rising full moon.

Were they praying or meditating? In any case, they were present. The Hindu monks sat and waited, as much a part of the severe landscape as its boulders.

Kim scrutinized the men. *I'd give anything to be even half as grounded as them*, she suddenly wished.

Saturday

My Reality or Yours?

That night the group sat at a round table passing rotis and small bowls of chutney and pickles as their curries were prepared.

"The inside of the temple was amazing! We couldn't get enough photos!" Beth laughed. "Did you see the boy swinging on a seat up at the main altar? What a strange temple!"

"The trick with perspective was cool. What'd you think, Kim?" Ross asked.

"It made me dizzy." Kim recalled dim light and a hand waving back and forth to flip a temple shadow from black to white and back again. The heavy temple air had been fraught with incense smoke and hidden portents.

Amused, the others waited for her to go on.

"I don't know what I saw," she said lamely.

"Bloody chaotic, wasn't it?" Gavin agreed.

"Crazy and chaotic. Man, Indians are superstitious!" Leigh folded a piece of naan and scooped up lentils. "Did you see the guy pretending he had a poisonous snake?"

"Pretending?" Kim looked up from her food. "The snake handler wasn't pretending anything. You didn't see the marks on the snake's hood? I don't have to be a biologist to know what a cobra looks like!"

"No way that snake was poisonous," Greg broke in. "Someone must've removed its venom fangs. Hampi gets too many tourists. A few snake bite deaths, and there goes your major money maker."

Nupur entered the conversation. "Kim's right, in a country with millions of starving people I doubt officials worry much about a few tourists getting close to a snake that may or may not be venomous. Visitors are kind of on their own."

Leigh frowned at her plate and pushed chilies to one side.

"Maybe little towns and villages use real snakes, but Hampi's a major tourist draw."

Ross served himself more rice. "How many tourists did you see? We made up a drop of the crowd!"

Kim took a pass on the goat curry. "What about the incredible drummers and the dancers who pierced themselves?"

Anna frowned. "You mean the weird guy with the fake knife through his cheeks? Yeah, I saw him."

"What do you mean, fake?" Kim felt more and more like a parrot.

The Dutch woman shook her head. "Someone painted his cheeks around the end of a fake knife. It was so phony."

"Those knives were real! I saw them up close."

"I agree with Anna," Jan nodded. "But, those swirling drummers! They scared me to death when I heard them."

"Heard what? What's everyone talking about?" Greg turned to Kim for clarification.

"You didn't hear six guys banging metal drums?"

Across the table from her Harry drank the last of his lassi. "Six? There were two."

"Wrong. I saw three drummers with one dancer. There was nothing real about any of them," Leigh insisted.

Greg shrugged. "I didn't see or hear any of it."

"I know what I saw! There were at least six drummers." Kim was stubborn. "How could you miss the noise? And the two men with huge knives stabbing through their cheeks?"

Bewildered, everyone began talking at once.

"Maybe you're right about the drummers."

"There was too much noise. I couldn't tell you if it was two or twenty. But, two guys with knives?"

"I saw a fake one. He was scary enough!"

"I didn't hear any metal drums banging, and I sure as hell didn't see any dancers."

"I was trying to find you guys. I walked a little ahead of

the snake handler," Kim tried to explain. "I thought I spotted Jan taking a picture of some pink cows being led past. Anyway. I heard this loud banging and red dervish-y figures with dreadlocks followed. Swirling. Pierced with curved daggers."

Harry stuffed his face. "A snake handler? And, pink cows? Oh, come on! I didn't see a thing."

"Everyone experienced different realities! We've got everyone's hard facts, and they only add up to why India's so hard to explain to someone who hasn't been," Jan declared.

Kim stayed quiet as the group debated the dynamics of crowds and eyewitnesses, arguing over what had – or hadn't – occurred. Hard facts? She relived a cold laugh in the air. What would the logical conclusion be if Kim mentioned that part of her experience? The inhuman voice laughed again, mocking Kim and her fellow mortals.

The next morning Kim dropped cards in the post box at the reception desk. *Goa was Portuguese*, she'd written, *and gorgeous ocean views, the rave scene and meals eaten in beach shacks.*

Cold and Hot

I'm quiet after he closes the book. Glen sighs and places a gentle hand on my nape as he gazes out at the road. I know he's imagining Hampi.

"Boy, if that isn't me and Janice and what led to our divorce," he comments. "That banging sound was reality's wake-up call. And everybody with their own version of what happened."

"At least you can feel, Timber. I read about a frozen world." Icy phantasms of polar light figured in my frigid tale; Glen described the spirit world of a hot ancient civilization. His tale is so, so much more in color than my black and white one.

On the other hand, our personal stories are as extreme as

any examples in Nature. His life is marked with fire and haunted by a vanished little boy.

My story about the Arctic Circle is changed by the situation I'm stuck in. I've moved from icy control to wild abandon as we try to reach Seattle and get back to normal life. Whatever that is or was.

Perhaps the present extremes are thawing me. Someday in the future, maybe, just maybe, I'll tell a warmer tale.

Timber's Best Stunt

The back road takes us through countryside and I drive by a field where blossom heads of gladiolas and chrysanthemums in gorgeous hues fill the rows.

"You look happy," Glen comments.

"I loved the chapter you read! Plus, Oregon's pretty. All the flowers... do you know they call Portland 'The City of Roses'?"

Glen stares at the fields of flowers on the sides of the road.

"What are you thinking?"

"How roses remind me of something I did to another person. Remember that first night when you asked me if I was seeing anyone?"

Without knowing why, I regret asking anything, then *or* now.

"After my divorce was final – quite a while later – I ran into someone I used to know. Kate. She was at a restaurant near the movie set where we were shooting."

"You mentioned her the night you cooked me dinner," I remind him.

"Right. We'd dated a few times, way before I hooked up with Janice. I had no idea she was in California. She'd been in the Bay Area a couple of years. We chatted, caught up, even flirted a little. Kate and the guy she'd been living with had split up and she wasn't looking for anything serious. She looked *good*. We traded cell numbers and the next week I called and asked her out. After running into her after so long I even sent roses. I don't usually do that sort of thing. But I wanted to reach out somehow. I wanted to send a message."

"Timber, how romantic! Women *love* it when men send them flowers, especially roses."

"Especially long-stemmed red ones. Everybody knows what it signals if you send a woman a dozen red roses. I knew she'd fall for them. And, for me."

He barks out a short laugh. "God, it was easy. She's good company, a *great* conversationalist, and we had hot sex. I slipped right into being with her. Kate's really nice. People think men say that and mean someone who's pleasant to be around, but no one you'd want to show off to your friends. When I say it, I mean she's a truly decent human being. Clean somehow. Honest. Oh, she has baggage like every other human being I've ever met. But she's candid about hers. I trusted her. I enjoyed her company. Except for one, small detail: she thought it was a relationship. Oh, yeah. I set her up."

"Timber...." The road's free of traffic and I'm forced to listen.

His voice is serene. "I'm not saying I did it on *purpose*. Most of the time I had no idea. The one percent where I suspected maybe I was holding back, I figured Kate was a big girl. She knew what she was getting into. I'd warned her. 'You don't know what a jerk I can be.' I told her, 'Kate, you don't know how huge an asshole I truly am.' About the fourth time I warned her she asked me to stop, because to her it sounded like I was setting myself up to feel like one. That's *exactly* what I did, but she got it backwards. I wasn't setting myself up. I set *her* and our relationship up for me to act like one. She didn't get it. So things got to the point where I was feeling something real, for the first time since losing Dylan. One night she told me she loved me, and I said it back. The next morning as she was getting dressed she said she could imagine a future with me. And then she said, 'I can imagine having a baby with you.'"

"So what happened?"

"I stopped seeing her. If I hadn't lost control I was in danger of wanting to, and I couldn't take that risk. When she wanted to know what was wrong I said, I'm fine. I asked it back, 'What could be wrong?' A few weeks later she got up the courage to call me and confront the situation. Was I mad? Did she say or do something to offend me? Was it because she told she wanted a baby with me? She was baffled. You know what I said? 'Why would I be mad at you, Kate? What could you possibly have done to upset me?' I got colder and colder. The rest of the phone call was pretty awful. Her voice had that quaver someone gets when they don't want to cry. She got real quiet, answered real politely."

Unconscious of what he's doing, Glen presses a hand against the dashboard. "I pushed it. I kept bringing up inane topics to make it clear who controlled things. I started talking about the next class I was teaching. Just in case she hadn't gotten the message, I told her I couldn't hang around and chat. Like I hadn't just done this shitty thing, you know? The best stunt of all." He stops and takes a deep breath. "That's not the cruelest thing I've done to another human being, but it's way up on the Top Ten List. I was mad at her, and God, I was still mad at Janice. I was paying back every single woman who ever messed with me and my life. I wanted revenge on everyone who ever broke my heart. And I was pissed, because deep down I knew I didn't deserve her trust. Where did she get off, assuming I was whole?

"The person I was the maddest at was myself because the thing is, I wanted her to fall in love with me. I fed it, I played her like a violin. Here was this sexy, attractive adult woman. Not a stupid young thing! She was smart enough to give me room even while she let me know she cared about me. I liked having someone in love with me again." He speaks so softly it's like he's talking to himself. "The way a woman in love looks at you is like standing in the center of the universe. It's the look on your face when I'm bringing you to orgasm."

My cheeks grow hot. It's true: at the moment of climax with him I think, *I love you!* How can Glen know this? Am I being manipulated too? I want to climb out of the car and away from him and this conversation. "Why are you telling me this?"

He gives me a bleak smile and touches my right shoulder. His hand drops, and he stares at his limp fingers. "Smoke and mirrors. I made a career out of faking actions, some better than others. I need to be able to say, I'm not like that anymore. But you have no idea how awful I was."

I don't want to sit a single inch closer to him in the car. A conversation with my husband comes back loud and clear: "Everyone's an asshole at one time or another." I hadn't commented upon Rich's acceptance of the label. Men.

"And it makes it okay because now you admit it?"

"How can I not admit it? That's the last time we spoke. I've thought about calling, but what's the point? All I could do is apologize for being what I'd warned her about, right from the beginning. If she'd even talk to me again."

What a self-righteous, self-congratulatory jerk. Glen's no different from Rich or any other man I know after all. What a letdown; what an important piece of information to keep in mind. The next time someone describes himself as an asshole I will surely believe it.

"Congratulations. You didn't change! The only thing that's different is that now your control mechanism is this so-called honesty. What a brilliant offense."

He ignores my nasty comments and goes on as if we're having a pleasant chat about red roses. "It took guts to call me. Women show that kind of courage a lot more than men ever do. I'd figured she'd scream and yell, tell me how hurt she was, something to let me know I was right, I *was* this hot mess. Believe it or not, I was actually looking forward to it; it was gonna be a relief. But no... after being on the receiving end of this crap, her one comment was, 'I love you, Glen.' In the quietest honest way, like it was all that mattered. 'Yeah, I love you too,' I said. Right before I hung up on her." The confessions won't stop. "I figured, screw you and the horse you rode in on. We men stuff it away and go off to brood. Lucky Kate, she stumbled back into my life at the perfect minute for me to smack her up good."

What I wouldn't give to watch Glen vanish in a pouf of bilious yellow smoke. What I wouldn't pay for that stunt take place.

"When Janice and I went to counseling, the marriage counsellor warned us about this sort of thing. He encouraged my wife to talk to me. Or so I thought. Looking back, now I know that he wanted *me* to talk, too, so that later I wouldn't turn around and punish some woman for events that had nothing to do with her."

I step on the gas pedal. "Why were your last words 'Yeah, I love you too' if you were being cruel on purpose? That would have messed me up more than anything else."

"I did love her. Part of me always will. It scared the hell out of me so I shoved her away. I don't want more pain. I've had more than my share in this life. I wanted to feel safe and up until last week I did. Then you came to visit, and the world blew up."

Do not Pass Go

I drive faster and faster as Glen insists on telling me things I do not want to hear. We turn a corner and almost run into a road block. The tires screech as I halt.

Soldiers raise their weapons in our direction, then lower

them and go on checking papers for the vehicles ahead of us. On the opposite side of the road, military personnel question a car of angry young people. When it's our turn, I hand over my driver's license and the car registration papers to a State trooper.

"Sir, I need your ID as well."

Glen retrieves his license and an identification card and I pass those out the window.

Across the street a young female with a pierced nose and orange hair stands by the opened car trunk, arguing. Dissonant jazz booms from the opened car windows.

"Like she told you: we're on our way back to campus," a man in a red bandana says. "We're students!"

They could be students. Kids from the Bridge Generation. Or cyberterrorists from a hackathon.

"The laptops," a soldier orders.

The driver waves her arms. "Fuck this! I'm a law student, and this is still America! We have rights! Understand?"

A female soldier comes at a trot. "Ma'am, in case you haven't noticed, America is in an extraordinary situation. A state of emergency. We're going to search your belongings, and are going to order your companions only once: get out of the car."

The young men sitting in the car burst into laughter. "You can't be serious. This is unreal."

"What a joke."

"Fascists," one of them remarks loudly.

What comes next happens faster than the time it takes to tell. In a coordinated action soldiers surround the car and yank the doors open. The occupants end face-down on the road with their hands tied behind their backs. Two soldiers stand three feet away, guns pointed at heads. They push the driver against the side of the car. She's petrified, and she's stopped yelling obscenities.

"This. Is not. A joke. You refused to comply and we are

arresting you. Understand?" The voice of authority is cold in the summer air.

I bite back a shriek as a hand thrusts my license back through the window. "Thank you. Your papers are fine. We're closing down all traffic in this area. You'll need to pull off into one of the next towns. Ocean Beach is closest."

"Can we ask why? What's going on?"

The trooper peers at Glen. "Maneuvers." He taps Glen's identification card before handing it through the window. "Screen Actors Guild card, huh? Would I have seen you in anything?"

I'm surprised by the sudden friendliness, but Glen answers equably.

"Just the back of my head from a distance. I'm a stunt man. Now I mostly teach."

"I met a stunt guy at a party once who did martial arts to stay in shape," the trooper offers. "You do martial arts?"

"Taekwondo."

"Earned a belt?"

Glen nods.

The trooper touches the rim of his hat. "You folks stay safe now." He points out the direction of Ocean Beach.

I turn the car around.

Several students are crying; the others are furious but remain silent. Two soldiers are examining papers and laptops. No one glances up as we drive by.

My shaking hands keep slipping off the steering wheel.

Ocean Beach

We're speechless as I drive to Ocean Beach, rattled by what just happened. The town hunkers down against the coastal winds. Ranch houses wear gray shingles, weathered and modest. The lots are filled with scrub grasses. Beyond the blocks we drive down, the dark ocean waits.

Saturday

We get a room in a little hotel, a dun building that fits the street. The weather inside and outside the auto is overheated, with the threat of a possible storm.

A family is ahead of us; we wait as they're checked in.

A television remains turned on and we all watch, unable not to. The footage is familiar, but the news tickers at the bottom of the screen give the latest details. The hackers transferred billions in funds from corporate accounts. World stock markets remain closed.

Everyone in the little lobby shakes their heads.

"We just came through a road block. They were checking laptops," Glen volunteers.

"We went through the same road block," they tell him.

We stand and talk in pleasant tones as if we're old friends. In reality we're a group of perfect strangers, trying to stay calm. By pooling shredded bravery and combining gleaned facts, perhaps we can keep the world in one piece.

I drop my bag in our room and without saying anything I take a blanket and towel and head to the beach. The clouds have blown away, and the late afternoon is hot. I wade out and promptly get smashed by a huge wave I never saw coming.

I'm soaked wet from the waist down. Far down the beach a dog speeds towards the waves. I spread the blanket out and the sand I smooth away is warm. I peel off my skirt and shirt and hesitate. I sigh, so loudly I smile despite myself. Good grief, I'm dramatic! I stretch face down on the blanket. *Go for it*, Teresa would tell me. I unhook my bra and lay it beside me with the rest of my clothes.

When I close my eyes the scene on the road returns. I'm caught in a loop. The protesting students; my girls would have rolled their eyes too, unable to grasp the earnestness of the situation. And the soldiers. They weren't menacing, just... deadly serious about their ability to search and seize as they deem necessary.

We lost time with the road closure. I can't think about a scenario where I don't meet my kids on time. I want to think about something else, and the conversation in the car returns. Glen's story angered me. I know people hurt one another. We take out our anger on others, on those who are blameless, on the innocent.

Glen confided in me. He admitted, "I am a man who knows the perils of love. I have dimensions on three planes and more." But I can't let it go, because I'm jealous.

I'm jealous of Glen and this past lover. I have no claims on him; our situation's beyond impossible and I know it. He said he'd loved Kate, and still loves her. What if she comes back in his life? I'm not considering leaving Rich. I can't tear my family apart. My kids go to school in the Midwest. I can't uproot everyone just to be with Glen.

I'm jealous of Rich and Miranda, too. Old scenes play in my head, seen from a different perspective. My husband and Miranda standing too close to one another. Rich is having his own affair. Maybe he's thinking of leaving, what if he leaves me? What then? Does that give me permission to go to Glen after all?

New pictures. My hands gripping Glen's thigh above a long scar he'd received leaping from a movie set's second story balcony. His fingers, urging me higher. My moaning as I come underneath his mouth. Glen inside me.

And always, my three children. *Mommy. Mommy? Mommy!*

I rest my forehead on my hands, beyond tired. My head's heavy with the weight of my continued lack of guilt. The fears for my family and yes, my husband, vie with the elation at breaking out of my own limitations.

It's too much. I sigh, closing my eyes. The sun on my back is a warm bath. The sound of the surf is a few feet away, lulling me to let go.

Saturday

Beach Wrassling

Sand sprays across my upper body and I wake with a start. When I open my eyes I'm nose to nose with an almost-grown puppy. The chocolate Labrador drops a tennis ball on my clothes, waiting for me to react.

"Ziggy!"

He ignores his owner and wags his tail. Animals always head to me and I'm delighted this, at least, hasn't changed. I sit up and reach for the ball – and remember I'm topless. The puppy snaps the ball but immediately drops it when I reach for my clothes.

"Zig!" the voice repeats.

Ziggy bounds on the blanket. He seizes a bra strap in his jaws and when I grab for it the dog tosses it away.

I reach for my shirt and the puppy pounces. Ziggy is way quicker than I am and nips fast at a corner of cloth, tail wagging harder. He knows we're playing tug of war.

Two young women point in my direction from where they're jogging at the water's edge. Laughter carries over to where I'm on my knees, hanging onto my shirt.

The dog snaps up more material and tugs, growling with joy. The shirt flies through the air. *My skirt*. I'm up on my feet on the blanket, bent at the knees. The dog bounds for my last piece of clothing. I try to wrap the blanket around me and clutch the skirt at the same time.

Ziggy decides the blanket is more interesting; he lets go of the skirt and bites an end of my blanket. He drags the last protective cover away from beneath my feet.

I teeter and all at once lose my balance.

For the first time I see the dog's owner, standing at a discreet distance; he's no longer calling the dog. Glen stands beside him.

"Glen!" I yell, but the two men can't stop laughing.

"Glen!"

He's bent over, laughing too hard to answer.

"Glen!! Could you help me out?"

With the word *out* the dog gives a last hard tug and races off with a purple blanket trailing behind him.

I crouch with my ankles crossed and my arms folded over my chest. I scuttle crab-like down the beach, back and forth between the spots where my bra and the T-shirt lay.

The dog drops the blanket and trots back over to lunge at my clothes, sure the fun is about to begin again.

At last Glen takes action. And what does he do? "Good dog!" he declares. He does three back flips over to where I'm collapsed on the beach. Glen peels off his shirt, his pants, his sandals, lies on his side and props himself up with an elbow on the sand. He wears nothing but boxer shorts and his sweetest smile. "Yup, nice day to get a suntan," he says, "pass the Coppertone?"

The Innocent

Before dinner we walk arm and arm down the beach. Dunes stretch as far as I can see. Inland, the hillside vanishes into woods. Wisps of fog thread in and out among the trunks of coastal pines and madrones. Twisted branches bend in homage to the winds sweeping in from the ocean.

As the sun sinks Ocean Beach turns chilly. Surf rolls in and out. The waters are ominous in the dwindling light, gray undertow muttering under the curls of waves.

I pull the windbreaker Glen loaned me closer around my chest. "I want to wave a magic wand and make this go away. Hide." I don't elaborate on what I'm referring to.

Glen gathers flat stones. "The worst thing we can do is stick our heads in the sand and pretend it's not happening."

"I suppose it depends on what someone's hiding from." I fuss with the hem of the windbreaker, eyes down. *Focus on getting to Seattle.* When I have it tugged an inch to the right I resume walking. "Sticking our heads in the sand is not the worst thing that can happen. The worst that can happen is when we let the crisis come between us. It's already a problem with perfect strangers." Vivid images swim up, men screaming in a supermarket parking lot, soldiers dragging young people from a car.

Glen's arm rises and smooth stones chase one after the other out into the water. "Well, the world's been warned." When the last stone is gone he puts an arm around me. "We'll survive. Humans always do."

"Do we?" I shiver, feeling bleak.

His arm falls; deciding, he puts it back. "Of course we do. Of course."

Smoke and Mirrors

The beach's brisk air relaxes us despite ourselves. We head up from the water towards Ocean Beach's shops and restaurants.

"What looks good?"

The catch of the day is posted on a seafood restaurant's outer wall. "That one," I point, but Glen's already at the door.

A brunette in a patterned blouse and a flowing black skirt greets us. "Would you rather sit in the bar? The next news briefing should start any minute." Through the doorway into the bar I see the television set hanging over the counter. Patrons drink potions of forgetting and wait for news.

We take bar seats and order drinks, anxious for the latest update as much as we dread what we might hear.

"There's a rumor the NSA is sharing their data base with allies as it's compromised anyway. You can see that as cynical or hopeful. God, I'd love to see it as hopeful."

"Who stands to benefit most?" a man asks the room.

"The hackers, naturally." The woman who speaks leans

forward in her seat and drinks off half her glass. "They named their price, did their damage, and vanished. Or if they acted alone, they still did their damage and vanished into whatever hole they prepared and got ready years ago."

A person at the next table jumps in. "But they didn't take out any nuclear plants. Even cyberterrorists know nuke clouds don't respect borders."

"Thank the Lord for small favors," a man behind us mutters dryly. "But the cyberterrorists are smart, they know it's little stuff that brings down cities. You know. Simple things: no traffic signals. Bridges not going up and down. Getting metro systems running again. I think they blew up a few transformers to get our attention. Like I say: it's the disruption to the normal every day that has us all fucked up now. Everyone's braced for the next wave even though it likely won't happen."

"Yeah, what about the implications for global security and financial markets?"

"It wasn't fanatics, just really smart people with laptops, that's what makes it so creepy, that anyone would do something like this just because they could. Or out of greed. All for financial gain."

Nearly a week has passed since the cyberattacks. The first shock has worn off, but life is off-kilter. We're all shaken. People are trying to be philosophical, debating cause-and-effect. If we couldn't prevent it from occurring, we want it to make sense. And I'm suffering from a sense of dislocation, of being separated from my family and home. I'd be trapped without Glen, both by the distance and my horror at a random universe. If Glen wasn't with me I'd sink in denial and nightmares.

Everyone in the bar is drinking hard. For the first time I appreciate the draw of alcohol. I want to numb the edges too.

We all look up as the screen brightens and a report starts. "Homeland Security deterred a group in Michigan and another outside Colorado Springs. In Utah an end of the world cult calling themselves VOG, the reformed Voice of God, joined a militia group. The two state it's their duty to take back public lands. They are armed to the teeth and have erected their own roadblocks at the entrance to Zion National Park."

I'm halfway out of my seat at the mention of Zion. Glen's arm holds me in place, steadying me. I yank my focus back to the bar and the continuing news report.

"And some good news. The Senate and President are expected to unanimously pass a bill to revive the WPA, the Work Projects Administration of the Depression era, putting people back to work."

The National Anthem begins as the screen goes blank. Everyone groans.

Glen addresses the bar. "Nicole and I need to reach Seattle. Can anyone tell us what's happening up north?"

A woman in overalls frowns, creases between her brows. "No chance on I-5. For some reason they're doing extra road blocks and security checks."

"You're best off staying put," another person advises. "They'll shoot down anything in the sky that moves. Birds, take cover!"

Everyone laughs.

"The government didn't have trouble getting the banks functioning again. Can you imagine the riots if the public couldn't get their money?"

"They'll never tell us how much vanished or changed hands. Smoke and mirrors," a man remarks.

Glen gets to his feet. "Let's go eat."

Not the First Time

"Any updates?" the hostess asks as she leads us to our table.

"Nothing much. Maybe later tonight." Glen talks fast. "I need a break." He thuds into the chair.

She sets down menus and rests a hand beside them on the white table cloth. "Take your time with the menus; no rush. My husband and I own this place, and patrons are pretty jittery. Take your time," she repeats in a gentle tone. "A waiter will come over whenever you're ready."

I've noticed this delicacy elsewhere. People react with aggression and nervousness to any perceived threat, or take the opposite stance if they can and respond with kindness and sympathy. As for me, I swing from rage to fear to elation. I force my thoughts away and study the menu.

We order clam chowders and avocado halves filled with shrimp. Glen orders sole with crab meat, and I want scallops sautéed with leeks and tomatoes. A glass of white wine for me, a third local beer for Glen. Alcohol seems to have little effect no matter how much we drink. And I was never a drinker before.

Before. Back in the days when I was a faithful wife and knew where my kids were at all times. Back when the world was one I recognized.

"Cheers." My smile wobbles as we toast one another.

We're diverted by laughter from the next table. An old woman leans over and kisses her husband's cheek. She gives us a sunny smile. "I couldn't help overhearing your order. You picked our favorite dishes."

"Oh, Grammy." The tawny-haired young female who says this and rolls her eyes is beautiful. She has the flawless skin and glossy sheen of someone with her life ahead of her. She's twenty, twenty-one maybe, an older version of Theresa. She sits next to a friend, who nudges her.

The young women slurp drinks in globe glasses through straws. I watch, amused beyond words, as they check us out. I can almost hear the category click into place: *Our parents' age group, probably parents themselves. The guy she's with is cute — for an*

Saturday

old guy.

I'm grateful for the youth at the next table. In a catastrophe you want your children to carry on, no matter what happens to you. I own a Crosby, Stills, Nash and Young album, with a song called 'Teach Your Children'. Its tender lyrics about how you on the road must have a code are suddenly, acutely visionary.

"...Keith and Sue James. And our granddaughter Cass and her friend Jolie. Cass always stays with us in August."

I come back to the present as they introduce themselves.

"Jolie and I are starting nursing school and Gram told us, if we want to specialize in geriatrics start with them. Grandpa got his other hip replaced last month so it's good we're here. But I'd come anyways. I love summer in Ocean Beach." Their granddaughter in the summer print dress and sandals speaks politely, but she and her friend keep staring.

"I'm Glen, and this is Nicole. Nice to meet you." Glen gives the two young women a smile that makes their cheeks pink like a blush wine. He's eager to talk, seeking an antidote to the road restrictions we learned about in the bar. "We had the best afternoon!" he offers. "We went to the beach."

The girls burst into laughter and for some reason it sounds familiar. For the first time the granddaughter's friend speaks. "We were like, jogging, and saw someone who was like, almost bare, fighting a dog for her clothes. And, you," she turns to Glen and her eyes go glassy in admiration. "You did this amazing series of back flips and took off most of your clothes too! When we saw you come in the restaurant I knew for sure it was you!"

With relish Glen and the girls describe the incident to Keith and Sue. I'm too embarrassed to do anything except nod. At the end of the telling everyone laughs and I join in.

Cass's grandfather offers, "We're on a budget, but we go out to dinner once a week no matter what. It's not, um, old folk's force of habit. Or maybe it is...."

"Are you from here?"

"We moved here decades ago. We love the coast," Sue answers. "Our daughter talked us into it. Lynn (Cass's mom), and her family live in Corvallis. We're glad Cass and Jolie are staying with us."

Keith says, "Lynn's anxious, but we're fine. We keep telling her, Ocean Beach might be the safest place in the country right now. And if not, then not. Life goes on, and that means supper at The Sea Shore."

"How can you sound so calm with the world exploding?" The words blurt out and I go red.

I'm saved by the arrival of a waiter at their table. He sets down two plates each of sole and scallops and in spite of myself I laugh.

"Okay, maybe it is force of habit...." Keith picks up his silverware and prepares to dig in.

"The scallops? They're the best!" Jolie declares. She widens her eyes and gulps more of her drink.

"By the way," Keith says. "Your question? This isn't the first time we were afraid maybe the world was ending."

History's Loop

Cass frowns. "You mean Nine-Eleven?"

Her question reminds me of Teresa and how glad I'd been she was still young enough that I didn't have to stumble around an explanation.

"No," Keith shakes his head at her, "way earlier. Way before all your times. In the 1960s, we had a total blackout on the East coast. No one knew what'd caused it. Information didn't get out as fast. No computers, and no Internet."

"It was 1965," Sue states. "November. We lived in Connecticut. We'd moved into this little ranch house, kind of a fifties bungalow, not quite a row house. A starter home, they called them. I loved our little house!" She beams with

Saturday

pleasure and places a hand on Keith's for a second.

He smiles as he enjoys his sole.

"It had three bedrooms which meant the kids each got their own room, and a long back yard. Keith hung a hammock out there and we had a picnic table and a grill."

"The kids were little."

"Lynn and Jeffrey were, what, six and ten years old? Something like that."

Sue nods. "They were outdoors with friends, playing. I'd gone to start dinner and the lights in the kitchen were out. The refrigerator light, too. I figured a blown fuse. Then our neighbor Irene knocked on the door; the Robinsons had the same problem. So the two of us stood on the stoop trying to understand what happened. Irene said, 'Shouldn't the street lights be on by now?' She was right; the streets were dark in any direction as far as I could look. Everything was. We realized there was a blackout. I called the kids to come in and get ready for dinner. I figured Keith could fire up the grill."

He speaks up. "Lynn and Jeffrey would've eaten grilled hamburgers and hotdogs every night if we'd let them."

"And corn on the cob," adds Sue.

I'm already nodding in agreement. My three kids are wild about meals outdoors on the picnic table. Louie prefers a good pork sausage to a hotdog, but he'll eat a burger any chance he gets.

"My Dylan, too," Glen chimes in. He presses his foot against mine under the table and gives me that special Timber smile. My stomach flutters and I smile back, our conversation in the car forgiven.

"Us too!" Jolie and Cass contribute.

Three generations represented by two seniors, a pair of parents, and two almost-adults in a fancy seafood restaurant agree: all children love summer meals.

"So there we were," Sue resumes. "My freezer thawing as I watched. Keith and I had a confab and decided we'd do a smorgasbord. Cook everything before it could spoil. To throw out perfectly good food isn't wasteful. It's sinful. And with kids we had a tight budget. Supermarket Sweepstakes was my favorite television show!"

"Of course, in the 'sixties not everything had shelf lives like today. Except Twinkies," Keith adds.

"Hey." His wife doesn't miss a beat. "Don't knock my emergency go-to snack in those days. Moms need one thing that never gets stale! So, Keith starts the grill. I seem to remember there was a full moon…. I made an inventory of what to cook. About the same time Irene knocked. The Robinsons had the same idea. How about we combine meals? I'd been saving two T-bone steaks for special. God knows when I thought *that* evening was going to arrive. Anyway, the adults split them while the six kids ate burgers and hot dogs. Didn't Irene contribute giant turkey drum sticks and we rigged an aluminum packet with those and a can of tomatoes? Remember, Keith?"

"Yeah, I do. It was messy."

Both old folks are silent as they relive the evening.

Glen and I are silent too. I relax into their memory.

Cass is fascinated. "You never told this story before, Gram. Neither has Mom."

"We never talked about it, not then and not after." Sue stares down at her meal and when she looks back up her face is ancient. "That night I thought, *the world's coming to an end. This is it.* Russia had invaded. Or Martians; didn't matter which. If electricity on the entire eastern seaboard went out, it was a foreign attack. And if my government couldn't prevent it, then I'd better get ready for the end. I was grateful to be with my family." She's somber, softer. "I knew I'd shield the children as long as possible. I told them the TV and radio didn't work, and how about we treat it like an adventure? It was really quiet, the full moon outside, the glow of coals in the grill out where Keith and the six kids were making s'mores." Sadly, Sue adds, "Our son died in a car accident a few years later. That was still ahead of us. The danger was the candles. I'd set some on the back of the toilet and on the edge of the tub so people could see to use the facilities. And we placed an old candelabra in the living room. Lynn bent over it and almost lit her bangs on fire." Her eyes focus far in the past.

"But it was like a party," Keith reminds her. "We were together. The Robinsons were our best friends and our kids were roughly the same ages and in the same grades and played together. If this was the end of the world, I was glad everyone was safe and well fed, I'd eaten a great steak, and I was with the people I care for most. Although if I'm honest, if I remember right, the steak had freezer burn.... And it was cold; it was November. But that's how I remember it, the best meal and one of the best nights of my life. Isn't that funny?"

"Funny...." Sue's voice trails off.

I don't know if she considers it funny ha-ha or funny terrible. Maybe both. Cass and Jolie have finished their meals and sit. Only their eyes move as they follow the conversation.

"We didn't talk about what was happening. It's not that it happened fast; it was the opposite. Information kind of trickled out."

Our own meals arrive, and they fall silent. The waiter leaves, Glen and I start to eat, and only then does Keith return to the story.

"On the drive home from work, I listened to the radio. And if no one reported it as a possible attack, that's what I suspected. I planned to keep it to myself and not worry my family. But when I walked in the house and saw Sue's face, I knew she was thinking the exact same thing. All she asked was, 'The city too?' and before I could do anything more than nod a yes the kids burst through the door to tell me about the lights in the whole neighborhood going out. We kind of looked at one another over their heads and it was parents' mental telepathy, as parents we'd make sure their last night on Earth was, like Lynn kept saying about the house being lit with candles, 'magic'. And, Jeff." Keith takes a big swallow of water and resumes in a low pitch.

Glen leans forward to hear, father to father.

"He wanted to help. Together we filled a bunch of gallon jugs and pitchers with water. Then the sinks and the bathtub. Later, when the kids had gone to bed, the adults sat with a night cap before Jerry and Irene went back next door."

"'I want to check on my kids,' Jerry told you," recalls Sue. "That night was the first time I thought of him as a good dad. Irene always had to haul him home once the two of you got going drinking beer or shooting the breeze out in the back yard."

"Beer drinking doesn't make someone a bad parent. But yeah, he liked his booze. A twenty-year old Scotch on the last night on Earth isn't a bad thing."

Sue turns to the girls. "Cass, you mentioned Nine-Eleven. In 1965, the scariest thing was *not* knowing. Nine-Eleven's a different story. It was clear pretty fast what had happened and who the enemy was. We used the information as an excuse to act out our worst impulses."

"Gram, you don't really think that, do you?" It's not a question; Cass is pleading.

Glen, Sue, Keith and I exchange glances. Keith and Sue sit up straighter. "Never get old people rambling about the past." Sue smiles at her granddaughter, asking forgiveness. "No, Cass. Not often, anyway. The East coast blackout? The next morning, I woke up and thought, wow, we're still here. Nothing had changed. But I was so very, very glad to wake up. Our story happened half a century ago... it feels like *more* than a world away from what's going on now. But it's the same historic loop: humans scared this time we've blown it. But," she folds the pleat in her cloth napkin, running an arthritic index finger along its seam, "maybe not. We'll pull through. And the important thing is to be with the people you care about."

"Excuse me." Glen pushes his chair back and hurries for the restrooms at the back of the restaurant.

Save the Recriminations

Keith starts a new conversation as if to mask the abruptness with which Glen left the table. "So, you two have children?"

"Glen has a son. I have three kids of my own: two girls and a boy. They're camping with their father this week. I'm going insane not knowing where they are or if they know yet. I can't even get them on the phone. We're supposed to meet in Seattle, but since planes or trains are out of commission Glen and I are driving from California."

Keith's eyes travel from the wedding band on my hand up to my face. "I see," he says slowly.

His wife's next words take me by surprise. "I don't know the particulars (and I suspect I don't need to) but clearly you and Glen love each other. That's not a bad thing, Nicole. You're right: the main thing is to reach your children. Save the self-recriminations. The rest will sort itself out."

I can't speak. I want to thank her and can't force any words out of my throat.

She's standing beside my chair with her hand placed on my shoulder when I can bring myself to look back up. "It's okay. It's okay, Nicole."

Jolie and Cass watch without blinking. They stay silent, listening intently, knowing something important has transpired. And with the newfound knowledge that it's important to understand, this evening the two have molted. They've become adults.

We watch Glen come back in the room. His eyes glitter

and I can't tell if it's tears from missing Dylan. Or being moved by the connection to these four people at the next table. Or the convergence of the lives and events leading to Ocean Beach and a candid conversation about the last time someone believed it could be the end of the world.

Keith smiles as Glen reaches our table. "After eighty plus years on this earth, the one thing I'm fairly sure of is that answers are seldom pat. And never what we first think. If only life were simple.... If this *is* my last night on earth, I spent it with good people."

We stand and everyone shakes hands, then hugs.

Cass hands her grandfather his cane and takes his arm.

"Don't skip dessert. Try both the cheesecakes. Nectar and ambrosia, I'm telling you. That's how this lovely evening's conversation with you two began: food."

The cheesecakes are indeed delicious. Glen and I sit and gaze out at the beach. Two waiters and a bus boy remain, clearing the tables around us. The kitchen door swings open and I see the wife of the owner, talking with the dishwasher. We're the last people left in the restaurant, but the owner waves us away when we request the bill.

"Mr. and Mrs. James picked up your tab," he tells us. "'Random acts of kindness, but no longer for strangers,' I think I'm quoting him right. We've shut down the cash register. You two can go ahead and sit until we lock up. To be honest, it's kind of nice to have folks lingering here while we're closing, that's the way the world is supposed to run." He raises his voice. "Stop whatever you're doing and come on out, everyone! I'll be right back," he tells us.

He vanishes into the bar. There is a stir as the staff joins him in there. Ten minutes later he returns to us carrying a bar tray with three glasses of straw colored liquid. "I got this late harvest wine at a tasting in the Mosel wine region a decade ago. Last big trip the wife and I took the time to go on. Since then, it's been all about keeping this place on its toes. They told me it'd cellar for decades. To tell you the truth, I forgot we even had it until a few days ago. I promised myself I'd share it with my workers one night this week, and here we are."

He sets down glasses and an aroma like fruit caramel meets my nose. He waves an arm at the bar and the two waiters, the dishwasher and his wife raise glasses like ours. "Enjoy," he says, and leaves us to head back to his staff.

We sip dessert wine and watch the waves come and go.

"Keith and Sue," Glen says suddenly. "Talk about grounded. Look at the way they reacted. Life carries on, buy perfect strangers dinner and go out grateful for what you had."

I think about it. Aside from the roadblocks and how nervous everyone is, things are surprisingly normal. Whatever that means.

"The end of the world," he continues, "maybe it isn't. I watched too many apocalypse films.... Look at this town. Nice people everywhere."

Flavors of caramel and butterscotch linger on my tongue. "The guys fighting in that parking lot. Militia groups taking over public lands."

"There are always crazy people. And yeah, nerves are stretched tight. No question. But for the most part we just want life to go on. We need normal. A crisis situation doesn't have to mean that we indulge our worst instincts. Actually, in most cases the impulse is to protect the people you love."

We're carrying on a conversation that goes back to Monday night and the initial attacks.

No. It goes back the first back flip Glen did off my family's redwood picnic table in our back yard. He'd leapt right into my life for good.

Glen leans over to kiss me and he tastes sweet. "Today on the beach? I could imagine some gritty sunburned lover, howling down the beach after the lost object of his affections. It's downright uncanny the way critters come to you."

"As long as," I begin, but I can't finish. I take another sip of dessert wine. *As long as you do too,* I tell him silently. *As long as you do.*

Sunday

Sunday

The Waves of his Ocean

It's long after midnight when we finally return to the hotel room. I pad across the floorboards on bare feet and slide under the bedcovers Glen holds up like a tent. I pull off my shirt and let it slide off the bed.

I move my hands over his body. This night we leave the lights off, and in the dark I'm hungry for him. I run fingers over his shoulders, down the muscles of his calves, up to enclose his cock.

For days I've been on the receiving end of his generosity. This night I'm moved by desire to please him, to give the masculine principle first consideration. I set his palms away from me on the sheets.

"Nikita. You're making me crazy."

My eyes grow accustomed to the light in the room and I make out his face. "This is for you." I lean over, molding his skin with my mouth and hands. His moan is a guttural sound. Both of us are trembling as I slow down my touch. I want to reach every surface of my friend, sibling in my emotional extended family, my lover. I want my touch to linger in his limbs. Later, when this is over and the world rises from the ashes or falls into them, Glen will remember. He'll recall this time spent with me, and his cellular memory will assure him I loved him.

Glen shifts his weight. An involuntary, low "God!" bursts from him, and the long waves in his ocean peak and break free.

Old Souls

I wake in a cold, unfamiliar room. Confused, I try to get my bearings.

I hear wheezing. The person beside me in the bed is old.

Not just physically; the entity turned towards me is an old soul with an exhausted consciousness. He's fighting for survival in a world gone insane.

I reach out my hand and touch skin that trembles. Over the sad years it has been ravaged by palsy, delirium, frostbite. Red pinpricks form and spread as I watch, the sorry souvenirs of breaking blood vessels and a body's long battle to utilize oxygen and keep the heart pumping. My god, the tissues could fold in on themselves under my touch.

The head on the pillow turns. Rheumy eyes that have seen more pain than they could encompass blink without direction. They're filmed over to spare their owner from having to face reality's terrors. Cords of ropy muscles stand out in his neck as breath rattles from an old man's lips. His mouth without teeth is an open wound. But his cheeks are a healthy cherry red, deceptive spots of color in the mottled features of old age.

It's Glen.

He recognizes me and smiles. He puts a palsied arm around me, embracing me despite the weakness of his tired frame. He loves me in this life and probably loved me in other lives, too. His limbs are warm with a love transcending all time and disappointments.

This old man in the bed no longer has the lean restless body I've come to love. The tired heart thudding inside him hasn't given up though. It will beat for me long past the day when the last blood pumps through its four cardiac chambers.

I'm washed with knowledge of how tragic and inexorable mortality is. And, the transcendence of love.

Glen's fragile body moves even closer. "Nikita?"

I wake up, this time for real, and lie in the bed still feeling the dreamed tears stream down my cheeks. The Glen holding me isn't ninety-nine and perhaps close to death. The man in the bed is forty-four and in his prime and perhaps close to death.

We're all going to die.

"You were so old! Your body was so old!"

Glen's eyes gaze confused, trying to understand what I can possibly be babbling. They're the same blue eyes of the old man in the dream. Glen's eyes have *always* been old, he's always simultaneously holding onto and letting go of things he suspects won't last.

Complications

Two sounds wake me: the closing of a door and the squawk of pipes as someone in the next room showers.

Glen had held me until, exhausted, I'd fallen asleep curled against his shoulder.

Light glitters across the floorboards and lies slant on the bed. I swing my feet over the side and retrieve my shirt. "I wish I could say I feel bad and guilty, but I don't. I love you, Timber." With those words attached to his name, I start to get up to face the day.

"Hang on a sec." He sits up and props himself on the hotel's pillows.

I turn to my lover and my smile vanishes when I hear his next words. "So if you don't feel bad or guilty, why won't you talk about what's going to happen once we get to Seattle?"

"How should I know what's going to happen?"

"It's easy, Nicole, you make a decision."

"No, Glen. For you it's easy. You don't have complications."

"What the hell does *that* mean?"

"You moved to the West coast. I stayed put and have to keep an eye on both my parents and Rich's. You don't deal with the daily hassle of coordinating schedules, or keeping from going crazy with the never-ending chaos no one else ever bothers to clean up, or argue over who's got time to drive the kids to Little League and girls' soccer and play rehearsals. It's just one big mess, all the time. Your world may be simple, but mine isn't."

Glen tries to respond but I don't let him.

"I'm not going to lie to you: my marriage is lousy. Rich and I would split up if it weren't for the kids. When we got together he wasn't aggressive about his job or power hungry, and now he's both. I'm going to meet him at the Space Needle because my family's the most important thing in the world to me." I sound defensive, which makes me even angrier. "How do I let go? What's the way to *un*complicate the situation?"

I'm on a roll as years of repressed bile spill over. "How about if your spouse has a drinking problem, alcoholism, let's call it what it really is, not every night but every single holiday and at every social event? I'm married to someone I don't even know if I respect anymore. It's great. I barely hold my life together."

Damn him, Glen goes to the one question I've been asking myself for days. "If the marriage is lousy, why stay?"

"I told you. My family. And a $150,000 mortgage and combined investments and health insurance policies and annual dentist appointments. Oh, and when we're home we have a date to go in and get Louie tested for hyperactivity. His pediatrician is talking about putting him on meds. A seven-year-old. On medications. So Timber, you go right ahead. Talk to me about staying or not staying. You tell me, what do I do?"

"I didn't know," he begins.

I turn away, ashamed for my outburst. "It's not your fault. I don't mean to take it out on you. Just the opposite. With you, I feel like there's some reason to get up in the morning other than to fill my duties to everybody else. I'm not cheating my family... I'm reclaiming myself. I know, it's selfish. I can't help it. I *like* the way you make me feel. Cripes,

I like it that I feel anything again, period!

"All week I've told myself, just hang on until Seattle, it'll all make sense somewhere along the way. It's not like I *planned* this."

"But what happens when we get there?" Glen insists, his eyes searching my face.

I'm miserable. "I don't know," I admit, and drop back down onto the bed. It's true. I *started* off grounded but have no idea how to resolve the proportions of the mess I'm falling deeper and deeper into.

The Sweep of the Minute Hand

It's a long drive up into Washington State but I-5 has reopened. Once we cross over the border we switch places and I take the wheel. I leave the coastal route to head inland. Driving is tedious but steady going until we pass Olympia.

South of Tacoma we hit more road blocks. Miles of cars wait as soldiers inspect licenses and check random vehicles.

"I figured this was going to happen." Glen retrieves his cell and calls his son, switching to speaker phone. "Dylan, it's Dad. We hit road blocks. I'm afraid it's going to take a while. Let's plan on meeting at 7:30. Go ahead and eat if you want. Don't wait for us."

"Dad. Don't be silly. Of *course* I won't wait. I'll be hungry again in a couple hours anyway. Hungry enough to eat a horse."

"Too true!" his father laughs. "One horse or two?"

And suddenly I hear my husband. Glen's tone is the one Rich uses, a funny mix of tenderness and light jollity, a dad's wish to keep his children giggling and happy and reassured.

"Three. Is your friend Nicole coming to dinner with us?"

"Right you are," Glen confirms.

"So I'll meet her again. I haven't seen her since I was a kid and her daughters kicked my butt in badminton. Cool!"

"Well, you've got the seal of approval," Glen places his phone back in his jacket.

Unlike Glen who drives with his free hand on my knee the entire time, I keep both hands on the steering wheel. Traffic in the I-5 corridor crawls through the check points. Something about these soldiers is different. They're even more vigilant, tenser than at the other roadblocks, maybe because these check points are on the main artery and heavily traveled.

Every few miles we come to the inevitable next barrier. Uniforms swarm over the roads. FBI. CIA. Army. Air Force. Police. *Rich man, poor man, beggar man, thief. Doctor, lawyer, Indian chief. London bridge is falling down.* Louie's singsongs chant in my brain.

A soldier waves us over.

"Papers." He scrutinizes them, and the car. "You two are a long way from northern California. And you live in different parts of the country. Ma'am, sir, step out of the vehicle."

I get out of the car and a second solider separates us. We wait at a distance from one another. I stand shivering. The eerie silence in which they inspect the car is broken by a ring tone. "My phone!" I rush to answer the cell phone sitting on the dash.

In a split second every soldier has their weapons pointed at my head. I freeze where I stand and literally feel my heart in my dry mouth.

"Please," I beg. I'm breathing hard, hands stretched in longing.

The soldiers keep their machine guns aimed but the fingers on triggers ease. It's another ten minutes before someone nods at us that the car is okay and I can touch the phone.

I grab it and see the name *Rich* on the display. I retrieve voice mail as my blood pounds in my eardrums.

"Babe? Babe," Rich repeats, "the batteries are about dead, I effing forgot to keep them charged so I need to make this short. We're okay. We're way over on the Olympic Peninsula, traffic's unbelievable, roadblocks everywhere and they made us get off the main road. Someone told us the wildest story this morning. We won't reach Seattle tonight. Tomorrow at the Space Needle for sure though. I hope."

"Mommy!" my children cry in the background. "Hi, Mommy!"

"You better drive," I tell Glen. I am gripping my cell phone so hard that my hand hurts. But when I dial Rich's phone, his batteries are indeed dead.

We're waved through another final road block ten minutes later and the flow of cars slowly speeds up. "We may get there on time after all," Glen says.

I can't tell if he's relieved or disappointed.

Glen and I drop our bags by the foot of the bed in the dingy hotel room. A clock hangs on the wall over the dresser. The second hand sweeps around, taking our time along with it. We have two hours before we meet Dylan down on the waterfront.

"Nikita." Glen's arms around my waist rise to my breasts and he kisses me hungrily.

What is it?

He lies in the bed afterwards, silent.

For the first time we take separate showers. I wash carefully in preparation for meeting Dylan, wanting to remove any whiff of illicit passion.

While Glen showers I stare out the window. When I turn around, he's getting dressed.

"What is it?" I hope he won't start another fight on our last night together.

He gives me a bleak look before he pulls his shirt from the arm of the stuffed easy chair in the corner and turns his back to me. "What is it?" He parrots my question from under the green shirt going over his head. "Do you know what tonight is?"

"Sunday night." I walk back to the bed.

"Right. Our last night together. Tomorrow's Monday and we go meet your family at the Space Needle. And that'll be it."

"I'm not thinking about that part." I run a hand over the chenille bed spread and pick at the threads with my nails. "I'll deal with it later." My nails are too long; I'll need to clip them short again.

"Don't you fly home in two days?" Glen's voice is careful, maybe even uninterested. He keeps his back to me. "Don't you have to go home and face real life, just like the rest of us?"

"I'll deal with it when I get there."

"You'll deal with it when you're gone. You've had a plane ticket in your bags the entire time. This time with me would have been one night, then it became another with a grounded plane, and we got a whole week of being intimate. I'm not the only one who likes things safe."

"This isn't about what I can control. This is about what I can't."

He opens his mouth and for a split second I'm afraid another argument is inevitable. It's his turn to go gaze out the window. When he turns back, a determinedly gentle look is in his eyes. "Nikita: Frenchwoman of my Heart," he recites like a mantra of his own. Glen smiles. "Ready to go?"

It'll Help You Both

On the sidewalk stands a watchful teenager with a nose that looks like it's carved from ivory. He's thin, with the

Sunday

tensile strength of metal wire like a hidden antenna.

Dylan spots my hand in his father's before I can remove it. A grin appears and the Timber of my childhood is suddenly present. He bounces up and down on sneakered feet. "I know," he tells his dad. "You reserved us a table, right? But I wanted to stand outside where I could see you coming. Dad!"

"Let's go see if they held that table." Glen's face is red.

Glen and Dylan banter back and forth. It's downright eerie how he resembles his father when he laughs. Otherwise, he doesn't look much like the boy in the photographs in Glen's shelves. His affect is too old for sixteen.

I recall the two young women in Ocean Beach and the way Cass and Jolie both looked so much older at the end of the evening. The current situation is forcing everyone to grow up in a hurry. I hope that's not what my kids look like when I see them tomorrow. I pray they won't be solemn and somber, like our changed world.

The restaurant tablecloths are salmon pink and in the center of each a large white chrysanthemum blossom floats in a glass bowl. Beyond the north wall's floor-to-ceiling windows are the waters of Puget Sound. The view is the only ornamentation the restaurant needs.

Something's missing. I wait a minute and it comes to me: the night skies are still free of planes. No jets snarl overhead. I'm waiting for the other shoe to drop and civilization to break down altogether. I expect the awful cliché of worst case scenarios. Things burning. Gangs. Looting. For the first time I feel a spark of cautious hope for the future. Maybe, just maybe these things won't happen.

Dylan sits across the table and Glen sits to my left. Dylan keeps grinning. Later, as we eat dessert, he declares, "Dad, Nicole, what's going on?"

Glen and I are sharing a chocolate pecan pie. I save the last bites for him, insistent.

"My own flesh and blood, questioning the fact that I'm happy to see him again. Why else would I drive up here?"

"You told me you did it because Nicole needed a ride." Dylan calmly goes on eating as he turns to me. "Dad likes to do stuff for the people he cares about. Don't feel bad, it's not your fault." He looks up from his ice cream and gives me the pleasure of a grin.

I like this young man so, so much.

He licks his spoon. "You know what you should do tomorrow? Go to the Seattle Center." Dylan doesn't notice me flinch. "Mom and John (my step-dad) and I went this afternoon. Dad, you need to go too."

Glen clears his throat. Underneath the table his hand rests on my lap. "What is it exactly we should do or see there?"

"You and Nicole just need to go. Promise me you will." Dylan stares out the window toward the dark silhouette of the Olympic Mountains with a faraway expression. But his eyes are soft, and they glisten.

Glen squeezes my knee. "If it's important to you, I promise we'll go."

On the boardwalk in front of the restaurant we say our goodbyes before Glen sets his son in the waiting taxi. Dylan wraps his teenage arms around me in a clumsy hug. "Dad shouldn't be alone. I'm glad you're here." He surprises his father with a kiss. "See you tomorrow, Dad."

Glen looks pleased but only says, "I'll call after I've dropped off Nicole."

Dylan rolls down the cab window. "The International Fountain's something good. It'll help you both." He waves to us until the cab turns the corner and vanishes.

"Let's not go back to the hotel yet." Glen takes my hand back in his and we stroll along the waterfront. It's eerie and still out on the Seattle streets. Totem poles carved from tall straight trees cast silhouettes in the dim lights. Wooden birds and mammals loom out of the dark of a waterfront park and then disappear again. They seem like magical transformed redwoods.

Glen's warm hand gives mine a squeeze. "It's strange," he remarks. "It feels familiar. For days I've been flashing on what you were like when we were younger."

"Sure of myself and where I was going. Focused. Grounded."

His hand squeezes again. "Yes and no. Smart, but way too encased. A little brittle. You're softer now. You've grown into Nikita: Lover of Life." Glen hears the sigh escape me. "It's the best part of you. That's why you're a great mom. It's the part of you that loves animals."

"It's the part of me that loves you," I say, and finally I can cry.

Later, with each movement of my limbs, my hands holding Glen against me and inside me as deep as I can have him, I'm making love to the reborn, reclaimed parts of myself. I still don't know what to do in the morning. I'm still Nicole, and I need her hardheaded strength.

But Nikita has crowded in and taken up residence, insistent that life needs to include more. "Timber," I moan. "I love you," I say, and my brittle parts crash. What's left is raw and tender, pink, like new skin.

MONDAY

Monday

Flowers for our World

He's awake and watching me when I open my eyes. He kisses my eyelids and begins to touch me all over.

I put my hands on him. We're trying one more time, perhaps the last time ever, to memorize bumps and curves and scars and wrinkles. We lay for a long, long time pressed as close together as we can get and it's not close enough.

He kisses my eyelids again. "How are you doing?"

"Lousy. You?"

"This is one time I can't control a situation and I'd sell my soul to be able to. But you and Dylan are the two people I won't push into anything you don't want to do."

I pull away ever so slightly to look at my lover and see that he's whole. It took the events of the last week and a reconnection with me for his wounds of grief to reopen and begin at last to truly heal.

We've traveled hundreds of miles through the extremes of stories real and imagined to arrive. Healed, here, we leave the hotel and drive the last road back to the present.

It's cold in Seattle, a gray day. I'm glad I packed away my skirts and put on jeans. The black and white shadow of the Seattle Center Space Needle stretches slant in the light of dying summer, an elongated pyramid. A huge crowd has gathered on the Seattle Center lawns.

"Timber, do you remember? Terrorists planned to attack the Space Needle in 2000."

He puts an arm across my shoulders and steers me towards the Flag Pavilion. His body next to mine is support rather than a lover's touch. Glen knows what I need.

I can't see much through the huge crowds. We get closer and there's a fountain in the center of the grass lawn. It sits in a crater, as if God scooped out a hole in the earth. The crater walls slope; the fountain is a high, silver-colored metal sculpture. It reminds me of an Arctic snow igloo, melting and bursting its surfaces. Or it resembles a barrel cactus in flower. Mist shimmers with a quiet hiss and the spatter of dripping water. Countless jets spout.

The bowl's a hive of humanity. Hundreds of people sit on the concrete bench which circles the perimeter, more visitors coming and going in a continuous flow. The lawns are covered by mounds of flowers.

Music plays from a portable boom box on the grass. Soft flute notes and the steady, muted rhythm of rawhide drums float across the lawns. Bang, bang, bang, they whisper. Bang, bang, bang.

Young men walk by with shaved heads and saffron robes. To my right a father grasps the hand of a little girl about Louie's age; the mother cradles a baby in a cloth carrier bound across her chest. Four women pass me, all holding hands. A group of bikers walk by, their faces sad behind mirrored sunglasses. Everyone carries flowers. Some people hold entire bouquets of tulips or carnations in their arms. Others carry a single long lily or sunflower.

Glen and I head for a flower vendor's stand. "I'm just about sold out," the young redhead tells him.

"What's going on?" Glen asks.

"It's a way for people to come together. The city extended the ceremony because more people want to take part."

"Let me get these." Glen comes away carrying two long-stemmed red roses. He hands me one of them. "These are all she has left."

"They're perfect. A long-stemmed red rose is passion, and life, and blood," I say. Who am I to talk about passion? But that's exactly who I am now. What's more, that's what I'm going to live by from now on.

When we go back to the fountain I see photographs laying on the ground. Many have frames, but some are in simple plastic sleeves. Solemn men and women in university robes. Pictures of small children, nestled in the plush toy arms of bears or bunnies.

"Look at the model plane," I point. "See the policeman's uniform?" It's all but disappeared under a carpet of flowers.

Letters and poems lay there too. We stop in front of each photo and hand-lettered message.

'London, we ache with you.'

'For my cousin Doris, gone in Kuala Lumpur.'

We read them out loud to one another, honoring the losses being expressed in this public way, this intimate fashion.

We follow behind a couple with three children. The man holds flowers. His wife wears a long cotton coat and a scarf covers her head. She has flowers, too. The crowds swirl and they vanish in the mass of humanity.

Someone constructed three beautiful bowers. Flowers and messages twist up and over the arcs; votive candles burn.

While most visitors remain silent, some talk as they walk along, pointing to a particular item. Tears stream but faces are peaceful. We're all trying to come to terms with the cyberattacks.

Children grasp chalk and crouch against the walls of the fountain bowl. Pink hearts take shape under small fingers. Alongside the hearts emerge the rays of a full, golden sun. A little boy makes a smile in the center with a flourish of the yellow chalk in his fist.

The giant bowl containing the fountain and the lawns around it fill with more, and more, and more flowers. Everyone walks clockwise around the fountain and then goes back to place flowers down in front of them onto the lawn.

Glen and I reach the place where we began. I want to choose a spot, but see that they're all perfect. We bend to place our roses. I drop mine from a height, but Glen stoops for a long minute with his head bowed. He lays the rose reverently between my flower and the handpicked posy a small blond boy just scattered. When he lifts his head, he laughs as his tears fall. "Tears are all right sometimes." He laughs again. "Sometimes, all you can do is cry."

We find seats on the stone bench, witnesses and participants as crowds offer up prayers.

I'm part of a ceremony of letting go and learning how to be grounded again. This story that captivated us began with anonymous hackers trying to bring the world to its knees. It ends here, with thousands of people laying flowers. All our stories are joined.

I lean my cheek against Glen's shoulder and we sit with our arms wrapped around one another. His long arm reaches under my armpit and I feel his fingers against my lower ribs. I breathe in and out and am warm where his hand rests.

I've never felt his humanity more than in this moment. With all his flaws, his conscious and unintentional missteps and mistakes, Glen is the most decent person I know. His strength as a man will allow him to let me go; our bond is beyond sexual intimacy or friendship. I know that if I decide never to see him again, he will consent, forgive, – and go on loving.

Reluctantly I straighten and withdraw my arm. "It's time." We stand and begin to cross the Seattle Center grounds, heading to the Space Needle. The structure's white legs cast long, black shadows, a pyramid that stretches as far as I can see, endless.

Swallowing hard, I take his hands in mine and press them tight. A kite flutters high above us. I spot Rich and the kids standing in a knot near one of the Space Needle's legs.

The kids wave, and I wave back. They break away from their father and begin to run.

Somehow I get the words out. "Thank you, for everything."

"Nikita." Glen's expression contains so much tenderness

that my already breaking heart shatters. He steps back and lets go.

I take his hands back in mine and look at him. "*Timber*," I say.

THE END

Afterword

This book is dedicated to Lou Corbett, X-ray technician, world traveler and photographer extraordinaire. He gave me a tour of Harborview's Trauma and Burn Units. Nurse Technician Monica Hayes works on the Burn Unit and kindly filled in the gaps. SnowWorld (www.vrpain.com) was the first immersion virtual world designed for reducing pain. It was created by HITLab of the University of Washington together with Harborview Burn Center.

Dr. Martin Klos helped with the medical descriptions. Nurse Administrator Liz Slater remains my go-to medical encyclopedia. Lisa Gingles has three children and the insights I don't. Jane Berger's editing always takes plot holes and my breath away.

My husband did winter testing of car electronic systems in northern Sweden. I flew up for a long weekend and this amazing biosphere stunned me. Much of my information on Lapland, reindeer, and the aurora borealis is from *The Arjeplog Times*, www.arjeplogtimes.com. The weekly paper is published by Illona and Johan Fjellström during peak car testing season, from December to the end of March.

The magic of the Nandi Purnima in Hampi, India is real. For a long time, it was beyond me to describe what happened there. I'm still not sure what I experienced.

Ocean Beach is a made-up town. This is my tribute to the name as it appears on maps of the West coast. I've always wondered why despite driving and driving, you never arrive at a town with that name....

The chapter title *I would not wish any companion in the world but you* are words spoken by Shakespeare's Miranda in *The Tempest* III.1.54-5.

The cyberattacks I describe are all plausible. Some have already taken place. *Schlachtfeld Internet: Wenn das Netz zur Waffe wird* or *Battlefield Internet: When the Net Becomes a Weapon* is a film from James Bamford, Svea Eckert und Alexandra Ringling, warning about the perils of covert data collection and control. Thanks to Nancy Carroll for bringing this television documentary to my attention. Nancy always has what the Birds of a Feather need, exactly when we need it.

I workshopped chapters and presented them at public readings with the Writers in Stuttgart. I'm proud to serve as President of this diverse and talented group. Birds of a Feather is my weekly writers' family. In September 2001, I went with a long-lost friend to the flowers ceremony at the International Fountain in Seattle Center. The sight of a hundred thousand flowers laid by peaceful mourners is the legacy of the Nine-Eleven terrorist attacks I wish to keep.

Jack Armstrong, Shaun McCrea, Sybille Müller, Amy Patton, June Piggott, Joan Robertson and Meg Valentine read and commented. The original rough draft dates back to 2002-3 and I set it aside for over a decade. I hope the gestation period shows.

I'm fortunate that artist Walter Share of waltercolors.com continues to create the cover art for my books. The painting on the cover is Walter's *The Brooklyn Bridge*. The country's oldest suspension bridge is the perfect symbol for both the dilemma and journey Glen and Nicole must undertake.

Lastly (firstly) my thanks go to Uwe Hartmann, with whom I get to explore the world and the contents of my own heart. A snow angel in the Arctic Circle, the sound of drums banging in India, and more are all possible because of him.

About the Author

Jadi Campbell received a B.A. in English Literature from the Honors College of the University of Oregon, and minored in Women's Studies. Ms. Campbell is a massage therapist licensed in both the US and Europe. She wrote for a decade as freelance European Correspondent and her work has appeared in bodywork publications. Her prior books are *Broken In: A Novel in Stories* and *Tsunami Cowboys*.

Jadi has lived in Germany for almost 25 years. She enjoys Europe's wide variety of arts and cultures, and has traveled with her husband across four continents. They've begun exploring the fifth. She's seen the Aurora Borealis from the Arctic Circle, watched duck billed platypuses court in Australia, trekked to Burma's Golden Rock shrine, and heard the tales told by Zimmermänner. They wear wide brimmed felt hats sewn with large buttons. Since the Middle Ages this guild of carpenters has traveled through Europe gathering work experience. It is a fine tradition, and Jadi hopes that travel and writing give her a similar skill at her own craft. No experience in life is wasted: each day brings the chance to combine art and practice.

She is still finishing a collection of short stories, and plotting her fourth novel.

Made in the USA
Charleston, SC
17 July 2016